DAWN OF ARIS

Also by Rae Lamar

Unlike Me

Somewhere In Between

Open

22

DAWN OF ARIS

a novel by:

Rae Lamar

STOCK PHOTOGRAPHY: iStockphoto LP

COVER DESIGN: Rae Lamar

PUBLISHED BY: Rae Lamar

PRINTED IN THE UNITED STATES OF AMERICA

ISBN 978-0-692-36161-0

~ *1* ~

AUGUST

Aris Collier sat quietly with her hands in her lap, watching the wiper blades glide back and forth across the windshield. She risked a glance at the man behind the steering wheel who had barely said more than five words to her since she accepted his offer to give her a ride. Beyond telling him to take the parkway and head north to Frisco, Aris hadn't known what else to say to him either.

Maybe the man was just following her lead.

Turning away, she focused her tired eyes on the bright white lines whizzing by outside her window. After such a crappy end to a crappy evening, she couldn't wait to get home. Crawling into her bed as soon as possible would be the best decision she'd made all night.

If only she had stayed home...

Five hours ago, Aris had been perfectly content sitting in the middle of her living room floor, completing the final touches on her latest mannequin...

Until her phone disrupted her flow.

She hadn't bothered to check the screen because the assigned ringtone had already given the caller away. Ignoring the first few unwelcomed interruptions had been easy, but then it rang again...and again...and again.

Dropping her airbrush, she snatched the phone.

It never failed.

The moment she found her rhythm and finally got in the zone, she was forced to stop.

Ralph always found a way to force her to stop.

Before she could properly greet him with obscenities, he launched a series of pleas and requests to come over to her apartment so they could work through their differences. Rolling her eyes, she had almost laughed. It was impossible for Ralph Jones to ever admit how severe their disputes and struggles really were, so he consistently used words like "differences" and "impediments" to disguise their problems and mask the reality of their dysfunctional relationship. Instead of reminding him of that fact, she simply told him not to waste his time and gas because she was on her way out for the night anyway.

That bit of false news was all it took for Ralph's urgent pleas to devolve into his usual, never-quite-realized threats.

Unable to endure another coma-inducing rant, Aris swiftly hung up, silenced her phone and decided she would go out for real. There was no doubt that her dismissive actions would be met with a week's worth of his trivial annoyances and petty slights...

But who knew that tonight would be the night that he would finally stop bluffing and hit her where it really hurt?

Aris shook her head in frustration.

Just thinking about it angered her all over again.

Snatching her bag from the floor of the car, she pulled out her phone and blew up Ralph's line. The probability of him answering was extremely low given their last phone exchange when she'd left the sports bar and noticed her car was missing from the parking lot. Name-calling and cursing hadn't been very effective, so this time she planned to try reasoning with him because, as much as she needed to be completely rid of his ass, she needed the car he jacked *a lot* more.

After several attempts, Ralph finally answered with much attitude, triggering Aris to make a fool of herself right there in the passenger seat of another man's car. When the show was over, she shoved her phone back into her bag, turned her body toward the door and stared out of the window, the remnants of her blind rage eclipsing the embarrassment she was beginning to feel as a result of exposing yet another episode of her ghetto, wireless melodrama to the man behind the steering wheel.

She really should have kept her ass at home...

Leaving her apartment was supposed to stop the stupid. Her plan had been to get drunk, eat wings and watch the pre-season football game. Alone.

Which was exactly what she'd done...

Until a strange man invaded her space.

When he introduced himself, Aris couldn't help but glance his way, curious to see the face associated with such a desirable voice.

Even his name suited him – Luke Donovan.

After a few more shots of bourbon, her attention had

easily shifted to the blue-and-white ensemble he wore and his solid body underneath. Lifting her gaze, Aris paused at his gorgeous face, the unmistakable look in his eyes making her pause.

He was interested...

Then again, her brain *was* soaked in booze at the time...so maybe she'd imagined it.

Even now, two hours later, she still wasn't sure.

Biting her bottom lip, she risked another glance at Luke Donovan before quickly dismissing her foolish assumption. His sexy, Cowboys-jersey-wearing ass couldn't possibly be interested in her.

He was *way* out of her league.

Still, that truth hadn't prevented him from going through the trouble of leaving the bar and returning the jacket she'd left behind. He could have easily given it to the bartender for safekeeping until she came back for it; instead, he chose to find her. He didn't even hesitate to offer her a ride and, when nearly every person passing by turned away after witnessing her erratic outburst, he had been the only one to approach with genuine concern...and *then* he placed her jacket around her shoulders. He didn't have to help her, but he did anyway. She appreciated that.

"Almost there," Luke said, reclaiming her attention.

She jerked her head in his direction, her mouth open.

Almost where? Aris hadn't given him her address. She had only told him to drive north before she got lost in thought. As he exited the parkway without asking her for further directions, she began to reconsider his good deeds and unwarranted generosity — from the shots of bourbon he'd paid for to the free ride she'd accepted.

There was only one reason why a man—*any man*—would be so benevolent...

Frowning, she came alive in her seat.

"Whoa." His eyebrows rose. "Are you all right?"

"Where are you taking me?"

"I'm taking you home." He shot her a wary glance as she leveled a warning glare at him. "To *Cypress Lake.* Where I also happen to live? So relax."

After a brief moment, she did relax...but only a little.

"You're not my neighbor," she finally replied after searching her mental Rolodex of fellow renters. "I'd remember somebody who looked like you. Did you move in recently?"

Turning his head away from the road again, he looked directly into her narrowed eyes. "For the record, I was living there *before* you showed up."

Blinking, she tilted her head. "So you already knew who I was before you bought me a drink?"

"No, but I've seen you around."

Accepting his answer, she pressed her lips together and kept quiet as he drove. When they arrived at Cypress Lake, she noticed that he snaked through the winding streets easily, like a legitimate, long-time resident. She relaxed a little bit more.

Pulling in front of her driveway, Luke let the car idle and unlocked the doors. She could sense his annoyance and almost felt bad about questioning his motives when he had only been trying to help her. Twisting her hands in her lap, she silently debated how to apologize for her negative assumptions. When she couldn't think of the right words to say, she shrugged and reached into her bag to remove her wallet. The very least she could do was give him gas money, but the three dollars and sixteen cents she managed to scrape up wasn't nearly enough to cover everything he'd done for her tonight. There had to be more...

In the midst of unzipping every compartment of her bag in hopes of discovering some misplaced cash, she heard him mumble something unintelligible and climb out of the car.

A few seconds later, her door opened.

Looking up at him, she accepted his hand to help her stand. She considered giving it a quick shake and saying goodbye once she was on her feet but found herself reaching out and wrapping her arms loosely about his waist instead.

"I appreciate you, Luke Donovan." Stepping back, she looked up and caught his eyes. "I'm sorry for freaking out earlier, especially when you were...when you *are* just being a nice guy and helping me out. I'd offer you gas money, but I don't have much cash on me." Her sheepish grin transformed into a radiant smile as a solution surfaced in her mind. "But hey, since we're neighbors and all, let me make it up to you with a home-cooked breakfast and we'll call it even... cool?"

When he didn't respond, her smile faltered. She couldn't read his expression, but it was pretty obvious that she should've kept her hug to herself and her idea in her head.

Just as Aris opened her mouth to ditch the breakfast plan and ask if she could mail him some cash later, Luke shut the car door and surprised her with a simple, one-word reply. "Cool."

~ 2 ~

Luke followed Aris to her apartment, careful to keep a reasonable distance. Despite the dozen reasons why it wasn't "cool" for him to be in this situation, he'd surprised himself by agreeing to breakfast anyway.

His evening had definitely not gone according to plan. When he saw Aris sitting at the bar right before kickoff, he recognized her immediately and figured it was a good opportunity to finally say hello. He had anticipated having a quick conversation with her before he eventually claimed an empty table to watch the game alone as he intended. Buying her a drink, driving her home and hanging out in her apartment after midnight were the absolute last things he would have expected to happen.

But here he was, still following her.

He had already involved himself more than he should have and he still didn't understand why she refused to file a police report, but that was none of his business. The only thing left for him to do at this point was make sure she was safely locked inside.

He didn't need breakfast.

He had enough problems.

When they reached her front door, Aris slipped her key into the lock and asked him to grab the large box in the corner of the entryway. Luke picked it up as she asked and placed it on the floor of her foyer. He could hear her moving in the darkness when she told him to close and lock the front door. Just as he was about to say goodnight and head to his own apartment, a soft light filled the room.

"Oops." Taking in the scene, she giggled. "I forgot about them."

"Yeah." Luke watched cautiously as she scrambled to gather the mutilated mannequin heads scattered about the living room floor. They were in all shapes and sizes, the apparent victims of every grotesque injury imaginable. "I'm gonna go..."

Aris stopped collecting the heads and turned to face him, seemingly oblivious to the rubbery skin that fell from the faux flesh wound on the side of the head she clutched in her left hand. "Why?"

He shook his head at the absurdity of her standing in the middle of this freak show asking him such an obvious question.

"Oh. Because of *this*?" She walked over to him so he could get a closer look. "It's my thing. Given your reaction, I'm flattered. This isn't even my best work."

As Aris piled the heads in a corner on top of a dark, thick sheet, Luke watched her every move. She began talking nonstop, her voice animated as she went on and on about what she'd done to her *friends*—Mike, Carol, Greg, Peter, Bobby, Marcia, Jan and Cindy. She'd named each one, having carefully planned all of their horrific fates. Then, she rambled about how embarrassed she was that her apartment was so messy and how she never had time to clean up because she was always working.

Somewhat fascinated—and also satisfied that this wasn't some cry for help on her part—Luke surprised himself for the second time in as many hours...

And decided to stick around.

"So where do you work?"

"I'm an esthetician at a boutique in the mall," Aris replied, securing the last mannequin before running the back of her hand across her forehead. After a deep breath, she strolled into the kitchen. "It pays the bills, but I don't *love* it. Honestly, I really want to break into film or television, doing special effects makeup or character design...or maybe both. I'm actually going through the admissions process for a few design schools, but I was thinking maybe I should build my portfolio first, you know? Or maybe I could produce a super low-budget horror flick and post it on *YouTube* to generate some interest in my work..."

Her voice trailed off as she caught Luke's gaze. He was giving her that *look* again. Only this time, she couldn't quite determine if it was interest or judgment.

She smiled uncomfortably and passed him a tall glass of lemonade. "What?"

"Can't say that I've ever met anyone who was into this type of thing," Luke replied. He leaned back, an amused expression on his face. "It's cool though."

"Yeah?" She shook her head. "Tell my family that."

As she thought about her love for the craft and how she'd ignored the naysayers in her life, her expression sobered. "For a long time, I tinkered around a bit on my own, building models with kits and stuff between classes, but it was nothing impressive. Before I left for college, I met some people in the industry who taught me the basics and shed light on the field. I hadn't been that excited about anything since…it just felt like something I was meant to do, you know?"

Luke nodded, his eyes never leaving her face. She had been talking nonstop since they walked in the door, which was very unusual for her. She didn't usually share so much with people for fear of contempt and criticism, especially about her art. But here she was, spilling her guts to a stranger.

It felt good…and surprisingly safe.

"Unfortunately, it disturbed my Dad so much that I eventually let it all go with promises of a graduation ceremony followed by a more appropriate career path. I can't even begin to explain how relieved he was when I finally finished school…"

"What's your degree in?"

She grinned. "Industrial engineering."

Chuckling, he stretched out and settled further into the sofa cushions. "So let me guess…after checking the box, you're rebelling again?"

"Yeah…pretty much." Looking above him to the clock hanging on the wall, her eyes widened at how late it was. "Wow. Here I am running my mouth when I'm supposed to be cooking your thank you breakfast."

"Hey, you don't have to—"

"Oh hush." She rushed to the kitchen and began rummaging through cabinets. "Listening to me yap all this time, I'd say I owe you way more than a few scrambled eggs and sausage…wait, do you eat pork?"

"I eat everything."

She winked at him and turned on the faucet. "I knew there was something I liked about you."

~ 3 ~

An hour later, Aris was loading the last pan into the dishwasher. Luke watched as she washed her hands and grabbed a carton of lemonade from the refrigerator before joining him on the sofa.

"Thanks again, Aris," he said, shifting the food around his plate with a plastic fork. "You're a terrible cook, by the way."

"Hold up." She raised her hands in mock surrender. "I said I would cook for you. Ain't nobody said nothing about you enjoying it."

After she topped off his lemonade, he took a long sip and looked at her over the rim of the glass before placing it on the coffee table. "So can I get some closure on your stolen car situation? I still don't understand why you refused to file a police report."

She snatched a stiff piece of bacon off his plate and ate it. "Can't report theft when it's not your car."

He raised a brow but kept his eyes focused on his plate as he continued poking a burnt piece of sausage with his fork.

"I didn't steal it...*sheesh*. Why you gotta go there?"

At that, Luke lifted his head and tilted it slightly to the right in silent recognition of her deformed friends stacked in the corner. "No reason."

As she laughed, his eyes shifted to her bare legs for a brief second before looking away. Earlier, she had quickly changed into a pair of black cotton shorts and a knit top while the eggs were burning on the stove. Her legs were long, shapely and much thicker than he would have guessed. He'd been doing his best not to notice them...not to notice *her*, but it wasn't working.

"Whatever," Aris replied, a smirk on her face. "So long story short...my ex kept the car after we broke up because he owned it before giving it to me. But the way I see it, he shouldn't have said it was *my car* if he didn't really mean it."

"He gave it to you or *loaned it* to you?"

She blinked a few times but offered no response. Luke almost laughed, imagining how many times that look on her face had resulted in her getting whatever she wanted, whenever she wanted.

"It's whatever at this point," she replied, flipping her hand in the air. "He got his raggedy car back now so that...experience...is over and that chapter of my life is officially behind me."

He watched as her eyes suddenly lost their spark. They sat in silence for a while longer, listening to the rhythmic ticking of the wall clock until he moved to grab and pull on one of his shoes. He couldn't let himself get caught up in another random conversation because it was half past four and sleep had to win out at some point.

As she held the door open for him, he told her to lock up. She nodded, closed the door and did as he asked. He made it to his car in seconds and drove the short distance to his own driveway. Entering his apartment through the garage, he disarmed the alarm and picked up the cordless phone to call Jessica. She was an early bird, probably halfway through her workout so he wasn't worried about waking her.

Inside his bedroom, Luke checked his phones. Jessica had left two messages back-to-back before midnight. One on his home voicemail and one on his cell. Nothing more than a hello and an expression of love. There wasn't a hint of worry in her voice, and she hadn't called again.

He wasn't surprised.

She trusted him.

Luke finally dialed her number, and she answered on the third ring. She sounded breathless, pausing her routine to talk to him.

Several minutes into the conversation, she asked if he was all right. He recognized the subtle shift in her voice and he sighed, rubbing the back of his neck. It was her way of asking why he'd been off the grid for the past twelve hours, so he told her he was fine and proceeded to share a few highlights of the football game as an indirect way to address his whereabouts and to bore her into changing the topic.

Accepting his explanation, she told him to get some rest and ended their brief conversation the same way she always ended her messages—with an effortless expression of love.

He sat quietly long after her face disappeared from the screen. Part of him felt compelled to call her back, to fully disclose the events of the past several hours but then he yawned and collapsed on the bed fully clothed, dismissing his uneasiness as sleep finally claimed him.

~ 4 ~

Aris was wide awake.

She rolled from her side to her back, willing herself to get out of bed and start the day. Minutes passed as she stared at the ceiling, rubbing circles around her navel. Over and over again.

She thought about Ralph. It would be easy to call him and continue their unique cycle of drama, but it was pointless. Their attempts to get back together never worked, no matter how many times they tried.

For weeks, she'd dismissed his twisted promises — to break up with her for good, to pursue other women, to report her to the police to reclaim his car. Blah, blah, blah. That's what people in love did when they were hurt...talk shit. Especially, when the person they loved didn't love them back the same way. So she had purposefully ignored it all. Ignored him. Never once believing that he'd actually make good on any of his threats, that he could ever leave her stranded with no means of transportation. Clearly, he'd had enough and was sending her a message that the days of him taking care of her — of taking her shit — were over.

She really couldn't blame him though. Beyond her standard loyalty card, she really didn't have much else to play in terms of their relationship...but at least she'd tried. If there was ever an award for Best Girlfriend in a Lackluster Rebound, it would bear her name.

She had done the best she could with what she had.

Didn't that count?

A few minutes later, she grabbed the phone off the nightstand and tossed it back and forth in her hands.

Should she call him?

Apologize and give it another shot?

Despite his demanding nature, Aris still believed that Ralph was a good guy. It was just his deep need for her world to revolve around him that annoyed her most. He had to come first in all things, and her ability to not get with that program was their turmoil. Somehow, Ralph believed that she had only chosen him out of desperation, once claiming that "fact" was the only logical explanation for her indifferent behavior and overall lack of energy for their relationship.

She didn't call him enough.

She didn't initiate sex enough.

She had never once asked him for anything...with the exception of his car, of course.

Aris never argued the point because there was a lot of truth in Ralph's accusations, stretching across the last two years that they had been a couple. Sadly, she really didn't want him, and he truly was her go-to resource when inconvenience surfaced or whenever loneliness struck...the latter being a whole other issue.

Fully aware that her fickle libido left much to be desired, she did her best to compensate in other ways but her unpredictable sexual temperament never failed to trigger the eventual demise of every romantic relationship she attempted.

At first, she believed that most men put up with her because she was nice to look at and a very good lay...when she was in the mood. Sex was typically an occasional but not quite frequent desire for her, always appearing suddenly and unexpectedly like a rip current. During the long lulls between her surges, she'd learned that very few had the patience to hold out for her next rush and not one owned the ability to provoke it. Even the best of them would ultimately see a hindrance where at first they perceived an ego-driven challenge. They all grew tired and unfulfilled in the end though, eventually taking off in search of the consistent tides of other women.

Hell...who wouldn't?

Succumbing to a sudden yawn, she placed the phone back in its cradle and left her bed for the shower.

Ralph was her past. She had to move on.

They both deserved so much better.

Stepping underneath the pelting spray, she took her time bathing, excitedly pondering the first steps into her newfound independence. When the water cooled, she stepped out and wrapped a towel around her body before wandering back into her room, her thoughts suddenly drifting to Luke.

It had been a week since he had been in her living

room eating her burnt breakfast, but she remembered every moment. The way he listened to her. Their easy banter. Those few moments when she felt like it was something more behind his eyes. His reaction to her art. His lack of judgment and his comment that he'd never met anyone in her line of work before...

She wondered if that was really true.

He even thought it was "cool."

Opening her nightstand drawer, she pulled out a worn, bright yellow folder along with a pen and strip of paper and began to write.

I have a unique and cool talent.

Bending and creasing the strip of paper, she placed it inside the folder with dozens more tattered strips of affirmations before tucking it away in her nightstand for safekeeping.

Satisfied, she wrestled her hair into a high ponytail and returned to the bathroom to brush her teeth and finish her morning routine. She only wasted one minute putting on clothes. Lightweight, comfortable and clean were the only wardrobe requirements for the tasks ahead. There were five items on her to-do list, and she needed to get them all done before her shift at the boutique started at noon. The first and most important item to check off was a visit to the DMV to get a tag for her new used car, and she planned to be there when the doors opened.

Glancing at her watch, Aris locked her apartment and descended the stairs to the parking lot. She had plenty of time to beat traffic and stop for breakfast along the way. After opening the car door and easing into the driver's seat, she inserted her key, turned the ignition…and heard nothing.

"You gotta be kiddin' me."

She turned the key again, expecting a different result. Still, there was nothing.

Resting her head against the steering wheel, Aris shook her head in disbelief. She bought the car only a few days ago. What could possibly be wrong with it?

For a moment, Aris stared blankly at the dashboard as a dull ache began to pulsate at the base of her neck. She didn't know a thing about cars. In times like these, she would simply call Ralph. He would let her drive his car for the day while he handled the repairs and, by the time she returned, all would be well—engine humming, car shining and tank topped off.

A part of her missed Ralph's solidity, his steadiness. With him, she never had to worry herself with problems because he always took care of them.

He took care of her.

She felt the dull ache spread to her temples. Pulling two small pills from her bag, she swallowed them dry and tried the ignition again. Nothing.

Her mind was still on Ralph.

Would he even answer if she called him?

Irritated, she yanked the lever to release the hood and stepped out of the car. She'd just declared her independence less than an hour ago and here she was about to call Ralph. That was pathetic. *Beyond* pathetic. Worse than that, she didn't care to subject herself to that knowing look he was sure to have in his eyes…if he even bothered to show up to help her at all.

Tapping the flashlight app on her phone, Aris lifted the hood and pointed the light at the engine. Nothing was hot or smoking, so that was a pretty good sign. It looked exceptionally clean too. Unsure of where to start, she grabbed the dipstick and pulled it out of the oil tank.

It was pretty lubricated; another good sign.

So, what the hell was wrong with it?

Leaning in closer to shove the stick back into the engine, Aris pulled back just in time to flash the app light into Luke Donovan's face.

"Damn, where'd you come from?" She jumped back, grabbing her chest. "Don't you know it ain't cool to roll up on people like that?"

Not waiting for an answer, she walked past him to try the ignition again. When she pulled out her phone to search for a towing service, he apologized for scaring her and offered to help. She finally looked up at him, her irritation dissipating as she realized this was now the second time that Luke found her stranded and cared enough to stop and help.

She laughed at herself. "I promise you I'm not this much of a train wreck…"

Grinning, Luke pulled his phone from the leather case secured to the waist of his pants. Aris climbed out of her car and stood next to him, openly admiring his dark suit, tailored to fit every square inch of him. Somehow, he seemed even taller than when she first met him, and his cologne was starting to affect her in the very best way.

She bit her bottom lip, thinking back over the past several months she'd been living in Cypress Lake.

How was it even possible not to have noticed him before?

"Aris?"

"Huh?"

"I asked where you bought the car." Luke's eyes were still glued to his phone as his finger tapped rapidly against the screen. He paused to stare at her, a grin on his face. "This *is* your car, right?"

She twisted her mouth. "Yes, it is *my* car."

He brought the phone to his ear. "Where did you get it from?"

"AutoNation." Reaching over to the passenger side, she opened the glove compartment and pulled out an envelope filled with sales paperwork and a business card. She handed him the card. "I just bought it."

Taking the card from her, Luke dialed the number on the front of it before placing the phone against his ear and walking a few feet away. A few minutes later, she heard him giving directions to Cypress Lake along with a few of his own specific instructions before he turned and walked away with the phone still pressed against his ear. Making herself useful, Aris slid the metal prop rod back into its bracket and lowered the hood. The sun was coming up, and she noticed that his suit was actually navy, not black as she suspected. She began to wonder what he did for a living. Finance, maybe? No, too traditional. She could see him in sales though. Looking the way he did, she would most definitely buy whatever he was —

"Aris?"

She blinked. "Huh?"

"I said the tow truck should be here by nine." His thumbs were active again. "They're already pretty backed up with the current rush hour wreckage."

"Thank you." She pressed the alarm on her car. "Well, so much for me getting an early start."

"Where do you need to go?"

"I can do it later. No big deal."

She watched Luke as he stared intently at his phone.

"Want to come up for breakfast?" she blurted.

Luke looked up from his phone with a skeptical expression on his face, and Aris laughed.

"How about I *buy* breakfast instead?" He smiled and slipped his phone back in its case. "I can wait until the truck gets here and take you wherever you need to go after that."

Pausing suddenly, Luke released a short breath as he reached for his phone again. He said his name when he answered the incoming call, but this time he didn't walk away.

She tried not to listen, but it was obvious that Luke was speaking to a woman because his voice was different and much more patient than when he was barking orders at the tow people. This conversation was more of an even exchange, and she noticed a hint of a smile on his face when it was his turn to listen. When his smile grew bigger and he suddenly laughed, she couldn't stop herself from frowning. Turning away, she tuned him out and busied herself with an imaginary ding on her driver's side door.

She was still inspecting her car when Luke ended his call. "If you need to go," she said, running a hand over the tread of her front tire. "I got it from here. Thanks for everything."

Clearing her throat, she turned away from his gaze.

Her voice sounded uptight, and the bitter edge that laced her words probably hadn't gone unnoticed on his end either. She turned to face him and sighed, once again feeling an urge to apologize for being so rude when all he was trying to do was help her. She opened her mouth, ready to speak...but nothing came out.

Luke observed her for a long while, a slight smile appearing on his lips. "I don't need to go, Aris. Cheryl—my assistant—has me on a pretty tight schedule today, but it's nothing that can't be pushed to the afternoon."

Aris looked away. "I was just saying."

He chuckled. "Go on in. I'll be back soon with food."

Remembering Luke's offer to buy breakfast, Aris bit her lip, feeling even worse about her earlier attitude and snippiness. "Thank you. Hey, wait...aren't you going to ask me what I want?"

"No." Luke replied easily, walking away. "I have a sneaky suspicion that you eat everything, too."

~ 5 ~

"What's this?" Luke asked, pointing in the direction of the television with a syrupy, plastic fork.

Aris pulled her eyes away from the movie long enough to glare at him with disapproval. "Nothing but the greatest movie...*ever*."

"Does this greatest movie *ever* have a title?"

"*Hope Floats.*"

Luke shrugged. "Never heard of it."

"I'll pretend you didn't just say that."

Aris turned her attention back to the movie and finished her breakfast. Not only was the food delicious, but it was also doing wonders for her mood. When Luke said he would buy breakfast, she had expected coffee and doughnuts or maybe a drive-thru sandwich, at best. Thirty minutes after he left, she began to wonder what was taking him so long and whether or not that Cheryl woman had worried him enough that he decided to ditch her and go to work anyway.

She was about to succumb to a too-ripe banana resting on her kitchen counter when the doorbell finally chimed. When she opened the door, Luke strolled in with two big, brown paper bags of southern-style goodness—pancakes, smoked sausage, country ham, fried apples, grits, bacon, eggs and hash browns.

Aris giggled at how fast they both tore into the food.

Yes…they were going to get along *just* fine.

"Ahh, she's smiling now," Luke said, watching her. "What's so funny?"

Before she could answer, his phone buzzed loudly on the coffee table. He blew out an exasperated breath and grabbed it just as Aris picked up the remote and muted the movie.

"Luke Donovan." Standing with his phone to his ear, he pointed to her small patio, as if asking her for permission and privacy.

She nodded. Then, he was gone.

Aris carried their trash into the kitchen, so she wouldn't have to hear yet another one of his private conversations. Even on the patio with the door closed, she could still vaguely hear the sound of his voice—controlled but slightly impatient, like a cross-examination. It was a familiar sound to her ears, an almost weary tone that she'd unintentionally mastered herself not too long ago. For a moment, Ralph crossed her mind and then her thoughts shifted as she wondered who was really on the other end of Luke's phone call.

Ten minutes later, he stepped back inside her living room. "The truck's outside. You ready?"

"Ready."

After her car was secured on the flatbed, Luke spoke to the driver before returning to his car. She was already inside and comfortable, staring out the window at nothing in particular.

They arrived at the dealership a short while later, and Aris launched into the business of scheduling her car repairs. After hearing the itemized charges, she managed to remain calm on the outside even though inside she was in a panic about how quickly her bank account was dwindling. Stuffing the invoice into her bag, she looked up at Luke with a tight smile.

"I got it."

Hearing Luke's statement, Aris rubbed her hand back and forth across her forehead. She was about to decline his generosity when Luke asked if there was anything she needed from her car before they left. She nodded absently, leaving Luke at the counter with the Service Manager.

Once inside her car, she grabbed her laptop, a jacket, and a few other items from the glove compartment that she needed. The rest of the items cluttering the back seats weren't important, so she stuffed it all in her trunk. After calling her boss, she made her way back to Luke's car near the front entrance. He was already inside, talking on his phone again, but he hung up as soon as she opened the passenger side door.

"You good?" he asked.

Aris slid inside and secured her seatbelt. "Yeah."

Luke tilted his head. "You sure about that?"

"Whatever the cost was, I can pay you back," Aris finally replied after a brief silence. When he didn't respond, she looked at him. "Maybe in installments or something?"

Luke eased into oncoming traffic, crossing a few lanes so he wouldn't miss the ramp to the highway. "They're covering it, so you don't owe me anything."

She blinked. "It's covered? But I didn't get the extended warranty when I bought it."

"You've only had the car a week, Aris," he said, staring straight ahead. "Fuck that warranty. I spoke to the manager, and they're gonna eat that. All of it."

"Really?" Her shoulders relaxed as she shook her head. "Wow. That's great...thank you."

"It should be ready around six, so..."

She watched as Luke pulled out his phone again, this time checking his calendar. She smiled, gently taking the phone out of his hand and placing it in the cup holder.

"I've already taken up half your day," she said, covering his hand with hers. "I will *not* let you put off anything else for me. Besides, I already called my boss and she said she'd drop me off at the dealership after we leave work. It's on her way home, so...I'm good." She patted his hand before pulling it away. "Thank you again. Really. For everything."

He leaned back against his seat, his eyes never leaving the road. "No problem."

Though it was approaching the end of rush hour, traffic was still pretty backed up but they were still creeping along at a decent pace. Aris was staring out of the window, bobbing her head to the music on a local station she liked. Luke rarely listened to radio these days, preferring his own music to the repetitive songs they played every hour, but he didn't care today. He was too distracted, reflecting on his heated phone call back at Aris's apartment.

Luke had been furious after finding out that Mr. Knox had met with his client this morning without him after he specifically told his assistant to reschedule it for the afternoon. Cheryl had called him in panic-mode and rightfully so. Though Luke had given her specific instructions, who was she not to concede to the CEO's sudden change of plans? Still, Luke was pissed. Not so much at Cheryl as he was at having been undermined yet again.

Then Jessica called trying to get involved, of course. Daddy's girl to the rescue. In a syrupy sweet voice that she specifically reserved for these occasions, Jessica carefully explained what happened and assured him that the great James Knox was simply trying to help. He was beginning to wonder when the lease on her father's *help* would ever expire.

Six years was beyond enough.

~ 6 ~

When Luke pulled up to the curb of the mall's main entrance, Aris grabbed her bag before he even came to a complete stop. She pushed the door open and rushed out so fast that she almost stumbled.

"Thanks, Luke. See ya later!"

Slamming the door, she tried to make it through the mall entrance before —

"Aris? Girl, I know you see me..."

She stopped her pursuit and swung around with a surprised look on her face as she faced her boss. "Kim? Oh, hey...I wasn't even paying attention..."

Looking past Kim, she noticed that Luke's car was still at the curb. Even worse, he had gotten out of his car and was headed their way.

"Aris," he called out to her. "You left your laptop!"

Kim wasted no time at all turning in the direction of Luke's voice. Pressing her lips together, Aris crossed her arms as he approached and shook her head at Kim's shameless appreciation when he slipped the shades from his face and smiled at them.

"Kim...Luke," Aris said impatiently. "Luke...Kim."

Tossing her head, Kim gave Luke a dazzling smile and reached to clasp his left hand in hers. "It's a pleasure, Luke." She glanced at Aris. "Now, why haven't you told me about him?" Kim didn't wait for a response before her eyes were once again locked on Luke. "Aris is always *so* secretive."

"Luke's my neighbor," Aris muttered.

Kim stepped back to give Luke another once over, her gaze finally settling on the ringless third finger of his left hand.

Glancing at Aris, Luke removed his hand from Kim's grip before quickly nodding his head. "Nice to meet you. I'll catch you later, Aris. Enjoy your day, ladies."

"You do the same...don't be a stran—"

"You done?" Aris snatched Kim's arm and pulled her toward the mall entrance as Luke walked back to his car. "You could have just slipped the thong off your ass and stuck it in his pocket...less obvious."

"Good point." Kim narrowed her eyes. "As long as you don't mind. I mean, I thought he might be yours, but if he's not, then..."

Kim twirled around, but Aris caught her arm again and redirected her toward the escalator.

"That's what I thought." Grinning, Kim winked at her. "Girl, you know you stay pulling some fine-ass men. Teach me your tricks, Oh Queen of—"

"I ain't pulling nothing," she said quickly, cutting her off. "And Luke's not *mine*. He's my neighbor."

"Right," she said, giving her a gentle nudge. "The can-I-get-some-of-your-brown-sugar-late-at-night kind of neighbor."

"Whatever."

"Ralph *who*?" Kim laughed, suddenly swaying to an imaginary beat. "Ralph *whaaat*?"

Aris rolled her eyes as Kim laughed harder, cracking herself up. Kim almost never missed an opportunity to bring up Aris's so-called magnetism and enviable list of Texas conquests—first David, next Shane, then Ralph and now...let her tell it...Luke.

Aris sensed that Kim knew the truth—that she was never as into Ralph as she led everyone to believe. And though that was very much true, Aris saw no need to confirm Kim's suspicions or share the news of her recent breakup with Ralph. Not then and certainly not now. They weren't *that* cool, and Kim was still her boss, who she would rather not have believing that her top-performing employee was a serial tramp.

Aris glared at Kim. "Don't start."

"I'm just saying. Ralph is fine too, but that damn Luke though?" Kim shook her head in disbelief, a sinful smile stretching her lips. "You lucky bitch!"

Aris shook her head, unable to keep from chuckling as she followed Kim into the boutique. "If you say so."

The woman in the chair was looking at her reflection in the wall mirror as if she was seeing a ghost. Her three sisters crowded around her, smiling because they had just had a similar reaction to their own reflections a short while ago.

Aris stepped back as they talked excitedly about their respective transformations. Though she always remained professionally detached, Aris was secretly thrilled that they seemed to love what she'd done. She had spent more time than usual with the women, affected by their genuine appreciation for her advice and the blind trust they had in her ability to "make them beautiful again." It really hadn't been that difficult; the women looked much younger than the half century—give or take a few years—they'd all been blessed to live. And now with her help, all three looked like they'd each shed another decade.

"You, my dear, are truly exceptional." Ms. Mary took Aris's hand in hers and gave it a long, gentle squeeze. Turning back to her reflection, the sassy grandmother tossed her head as her sisters cackled and crowded around for a group hug. Aris stepped back to give them space, but she was quickly pulled into the fold.

After several selfies and a group photo, the women paid Aris and tossed in an extraordinary tip. Grateful for the extra cash, she gave each sister another hug and asked them to stop by again any time. When she passed them her business card, Ms. Mary asked if she hosted private events or parties. Though Aris hadn't done it in a while, she jumped at the chance. Her recent car purchase had been in cash and had put a serious dent in her reserves. She could use all the extra money she could make; the more work in cue, the better.

"Good work." Kim came over and waved goodbye to the women as they left the boutique. "Keep it up, and I may have to promote you."

"To what?" She tilted her head. "More work with the same pay? I'll pass, thank you very much."

"You never know. You could be me one day."

Taking off her smock, Aris gave Kim the side eye.

Kim laughed. "I'll try not to take that personally. You ready to go?"

"Yeah. Let me clean all this up and we're out. Fifteen minutes, tops."

Twenty minutes later, Kim and Aris were strolling through the mall, ducking in and out of stores for some impromptu shopping. Actually, Kim insisted Aris help her find the perfect dress for a concert she had tickets for the following weekend. Given their tastes were completely different, Aris found herself wandering to the other end of the store and Kim eventually found her in the jewelry section.

"What do you think?" Kim held up two dresses.

"Slutty."

"Try them on."

"No. I don't need a dress." Aris picked up another bracelet from the clearance rack.

"Come on. Humor me." Kim shoved them into her arms. "I don't want to try on stuff alone."

Minutes later, Aris was posing in front of the full length mirror just outside of her oversized dressing room. She ran a hand over the smooth fabric and smiled. Then, her eyes caught the price on the tag and the thrill was gone.

"Let me see!" Kim strutted out of her own dressing room in a form-fitting strapless dress. She looked Aris up and down and smiled brightly. "Oooh, I *love* it."

"I did too until I saw the price."

Kim grabbed the tag and twisted her mouth. "It's not that much. It's on sale."

"I don't need a dress, Kim."

"You *do* need a dress, Aris. You need *this* dress because this dress is hot!"

Aris rolled her eyes, returning to her dressing room.

When they arrived at the register, Aris was surprised when Kim bought both dresses anyway and presented them to her as a gift.

"Kim—"

"I will hear nothing of it." Kim smiled. "You do great work, and it's my way of saying thank you."

"That's very kind. Thanks." Aris accepted the dress bag and gave Kim a hug, biting back the urge to tell her that a bonus check would have been a better choice. "But seriously...what the hell am I going to do with these dresses?"

Kim's eyes lit up.

"*Don't start*," Aris said, putting a stop to whatever nonsense was about to come out of Kim's mouth.

Kim laughed and followed Aris out of the store. "Brown sugah, baaaby...I'm just saying."

"Change the subject. Right now."

"Fine," Kim replied, still amused. "Actually, I need a huge favor."

"Ah. I knew those dresses had a purpose."

Kim rolled her eyes. "I'm having a fundraiser for my squad next weekend, and we need as much help as we can get to pull this off."

"Doing what exactly?"

"Raising money." They crossed the street and

continued walking toward Kim's' car. "We're going to post up at a well-traveled street corner, go car-to-car, collect cash from strangers—"

Aris raised an eyebrow. "I really hope you don't pitch like that to all your potential volunteers."

"Anyway...we're just doing what the firemen do. Instead of collecting money in boots, we'll be collecting money in these cute toy megaphones I bought." Kim nudged her before pressing a button on her remote to unlock her car. "Come on...the girls will be so bummed if you don't show up. They ask about you all the time. You know they love you."

"Well, they can love me when I paint their faces for homecoming this year. That's all I got."

"It's only for a few hours, Aris...please? My girls have a real shot at the championship this year, and I really need the support. The parents are tapped out, and the school barely gives a shit even though they'll be the first to take credit when we win." She stepped closer with an earnest expression on her face, staring Aris directly in the eyes. "Seriously, I need you. We need you. Your community needs you."

"Emotional blackmail? Really?"

Kim shrugged. "It's all *I* got."

"Ugh. Fine."

"Yay!" Kim clapped her hands before wrapping her arms around Aris. They hugged tightly for a moment before Aris playfully pushed Kim away. After they secured their dress bags in the back seat, they ducked into the car and left the mall.

After snaking through rush-hour traffic, they arrived at the dealership closer to seven p.m., which was good timing because the repairs took longer than expected. Kim insisted on waiting with her in the lobby, drinking stale coffee until a technician finally alerted them that Aris's car was washed and parked out front.

Kim drove out of the dealership and onto the parkway with Aris following close behind. After a few miles, Aris heard her cell phone sounding off. When she pulled it from her bag, Kim's face was on the screen. After pressing the speaker button, Aris brought the phone to her ear and looked up just in time to see Kim's car get t-boned by a speeding SUV.

~ 7 ~

SEPTEMBER

Luke sat back in his chair, massaging his temples. He had some reports to review, but his eyes kept drifting to the faceless, glass clock sitting on the edge of his desk. It was a unique piece of art, a gift from Jessica last year when he was tapped to become Executive Director of Product Development shortly after she was named Vice President of Strategic Partnerships. He frowned, glaring at its diamond-set, platinum hands.

Another half hour had passed.

And still…no response from Aris.

Luke had sent her a brief text as soon as he arrived to work. The last message he had received from Aris told him she was on her way to see Kim. That was two weeks ago.

The last time he had actually spoken to her was the night of the accident. Aris answered the phone, out of breath, telling him that she was at the hospital. Without thinking, he'd jumped out of bed and grabbed his keys, pausing only after she further explained that it was Kim who'd had the accident and that she was shaken but safe. Relief washed over him at the news. For a moment, he felt like shit because another person's life was in limbo but all he cared to know was that it wasn't Aris who was hurt.

Having such a reaction about a woman he barely knew disturbed him, so Luke pushed it all to the back of his mind and listened as she shared the details of the accident. Kim's family had arrived an hour earlier, impatiently awaiting news from the hospital staff on the surgery and Kim's overall condition. Aris had sounded on edge, saying it was her fault...that if she hadn't asked for a ride to the dealership, Kim would have never been hurt.

Luke had tried getting a word in, but Aris was talking too fast and then she was gone. At first, it seemed like the call dropped; signals were always bad in hospitals. He called back a few times, but she didn't answer. A second after his last call, she sent him a text.

Can't talk right now.

So he stopped calling, catching her sporadic texts and wondering when he might hear her voice again.

The words and graphs on the report were blurring together again and Luke blinked, his eyes drifting back to the clock. He wanted to call her but figured if Aris wanted to talk then she would have called him or at least responded to his texts by now. The fact that he was the only one initiating contact—stopping by her place, calling her, texting her—was an obvious sign. She hadn't answered her door or returned his messages in days. He needed to take the hint and fall back if, in fact, those were hints. Luke was genuinely concerned but perhaps she was misinterpreting his persistence. It was clear to him that Aris wasn't looking for more than a casual friendship and he was...what?

What *was* he looking for?

Leaning back in his chair, he pulled out his phone, glanced at the screen and laughed at himself...and the truth behind his actions.

He needed to get his shit together.

When the hell had his mild interest in Aris shifted to something more? In the beginning, she'd barely caught his eye. He'd seen her around, but there were dozens of pretty women in the neighborhood. Yet, she was the one who always shifted his attention. It was just something about her...but his curiosity was fleeting and never enough to make him go out of his way to say hello or want to know her name...

Until he saw her at the sports bar.

That urge to finally speak to her had surfaced out of nowhere, but everything afterwards had been completely driven by her. He'd simply gone along for the ride—from the botched breakfast at her apartment to her decision to upgrade them from neighbors to friends.

Luke smiled as he remembered the first time she called his place. He had gotten home late and saw he had a few messages. He figured they were from his mother and Jessica, the only two people who insisted on calling him at home before trying to reach him on his cell. He was right, of course. The second and third messages were from his mother and Jessica, but it was the first one that surprised him—a long message that was left around the time he'd left Aris's apartment earlier that same day to grab food before the tow truck arrived to haul off her car.

"Hey, it's me. Aris. I got your number out of the community directory...who knew the day would come when I would actually find myself using this thing? Anyway, I was just thinking...not too many people know that I have mutilated heads in my apartment, I'm a lousy cook and I eat like a man. In my mind, that makes you a friend...which means you get to have the number to my Droid. My land line is really only for bill collectors, but I see they listed it in this directory despite my request for them not to. The nerve...I ought to write a nice-nasty letter to the property manager about this...anyway, what was I sayin'? Oh yeah, my number...save it..."

Luke shook his head at the memory, grinning at how she could go from dismissive in one minute to declaring them friends shortly after. That night, he'd saved her number in his phone without hesitation. Instead of Aris, he had entered Moody as the name to appear in his Contacts list.

Straightening up in his chair, he put his phone away and shifted his gaze to the report in front of him that he didn't care to read...grinning, still thinking of her...

Yeah.

Moody suited her perfectly.

Too bad he couldn't label what he was feeling just as easily. Her effect on him was baffling. Not that she wasn't attractive to him. She was just different from the flashier women he preferred, women who were obsessed with hair, clothes, jewelry and makeup. Women like Jessica who not only knew they were gorgeous but reveled in it.

Aris was the opposite. A beautiful mess. Never once had Luke seen her thick mass of hair in anything more than a sloppy ponytail or just...*hanging* there. And her clothes? Just as forgettable.

Giving up on his report, Luke turned his chair and peered out of the window at the sky, envisioning Aris and imagining endless possibilities.

The desk phone buzzed.

Luke's swung around to check the caller display and then snatched the handset from its base.

It was Jessica.

She'd just left the lobby and was on her way up to his office.

Luke hung up and placed a hand over his mouth, slowly pulling it down his face. Frowning, he pressed the same hand to his crotch and purposefully shifted his thoughts to Jessica's father to quickly minimize his sudden... problem.

He *really* needed to get his shit together.

When Jessica arrived, he stood to greet her. She closed his door and immediately gave him a kiss, slipping her tongue into his mouth to let him know she was in a playful mood. Rubbing a hand over his dick, she smiled against his lips when she felt it jump.

Still kissing, Luke let her pull his jacket off and push him against an adjacent wall. But he had other ideas. Picking her up, he walked over to his desk and sat her ass on the edge near the glass clock. She opened her legs for him, reaching for his belt to pull him closer. They both felt his cell phone buzz, but Luke ignored it, burying his hands in her hair and covering her mouth with his once again. But the buzzing returned and Jessica stiffened, placing a gentle hand on his chest.

"Don't you need to get that?"

Luke shook his head impatiently, his eyes focused on Jessica's mouth. He leaned in to capture her lips again, but Jessica quickly shifted out of his reach.

"You should at least check it," she said, trying to slow her breathing. "It could be Daddy."

Luke looked at her, pressing his lips together as his erection quickly subsided for the second time in ten minutes.

Instead of checking his phone right away as she asked, he stepped back from her and grabbed his jacket off the floor. When he finally looked at her, she was calmly staring back at him, as if she hadn't been spread open on his desk with his dick in her hand a few minutes ago. Even her hair and clothing were perfect again, showing no trace of the charged woman who walked through his office door, as if the switch to her emotions had been flipped from ON to OFF.

Grinding his teeth, Luke walked over to his chair and sat down. The blue light on his phone was blinking now, indicating a new message. He ran a thumb over the screen and stared at the name of his missed caller just as Jessica eased her ass into his lap.

She moved her head lower to get a closer look before she casually pointed a perfectly manicured nail at the screen. "Who's Moody?"

knock. knock. knock.

"Come in!" Luke called out, happy for the sudden interruption.

Devin Jones strolled in with a huge smile on his face, observing the cozy moment. "Get a room."

Jessica stood and returned Devin's smile before walking over to give him a hug. "Jealous much?"

He chuckled, kissing her cheek. "Of what? The trappings of monogamy? Jessica, please...not at all."

"Well, when you're ready, I have the perfect woman for you." Jessica turned to Luke, closing the door behind her. "I'll leave you two to chat."

Devin gave Luke a once over and sat in front of his friend and frat brother. "You look like shit, man."

Luke leaned back and ran a hand over the top of his head. "Guess I haven't been sleeping much lately."

"After all these years, you two are still hot for each other." Devin grinned. "There are worse problems."

Luke shook his head. "I'm talking about work, man. But I'd be lying if I said Jessica didn't have a little something to do with my fatigue, too."

"Yeah, I've been sensing that things are about to ramp up. That's actually what I came up here to talk to you about."

"Cool. You ate yet?"

"Just got out of a three-hour meeting. I'm starving."

Luke pushed back from his desk. "Let's grab some food. We can talk on the way."

Luke and Devin traded updates during the drive to

their favorite restaurant. Devin was still fairly new in his role as Director of Business Development at Knox Corp, but he was already proving himself to be an invaluable addition to the leadership team.

Since undergrad, Devin had always been determined to maintain an entrepreneurial existence. And he had succeeded only until recently when he'd accepted his corporate role at Knox. After graduation, Devin launched his own small IT company in Atlanta. He was passionate, but also very inexperienced, which led him to sell his business for a lot less than it was worth. Devin worked as a consultant for the next few years, which was what he was now doing for Knox Corp. But the premature decision of his youth still haunted him, and he worked tirelessly to launch another business that was even more remarkable than the one he'd sold too soon.

Mr. Knox had been more than pleased with Devin's performance thus far, and Luke was happy to have him as his right-hand while he got the new Knox Technology Division up and running. It felt like undergrad all over again—Jessica, Luke and Devin with their big ideas and even bigger egos, ready to rule the world.

"It's a lot of travel involved, but not for a few more weeks," Luke said to Devin as they followed the hostess to the open booth in the best section of the restaurant.

"You say that like it's a problem." Devin replied, sliding across the leather bench and placing the dark napkin in his lap. "The further away, the better, if you ask me."

Before Luke could reply, Devin reached for his phone to answer an incoming call. Luke reached for his own phone to finally check Aris's voicemail message.

It was short and to the point.

He listened carefully as she informed him that she had been working a lot but she was all right. Then, she thanked him for calling. Nothing more, nothing less.

Without pause, Luke played the message a second time and then a third. To say he expected more was an understatement. What did it even mean? I'm good, stop calling? Her voice sounded drained, almost depressed. He wanted to talk to her, to make sure that she really was all right.

"Damn, man," Devin said, watching Luke. "If it's that bad, that's what vacation days are for."

Luke locked his phone and slipped it back into its case on his waist. For a brief moment, he considered telling Devin about Aris. He was feeling out of control, and he needed a voice of reason. But what would he say? There was nothing to tell. He met a girl, and now she was blatantly blowing him off. Case closed.

"You and Jess need to take a week off or something," Devin continued. "Get some rest and clear your head. The two months off that I had before starting Knox was the best thing I could've done for myself. I didn't even know I needed it until after I literally slept the whole first week. There's nothing wrong with going hard, but downtime is a must, dude. Trust me. That burnout shit is nothing to play with."

Taking a sip of water, Luke admitted to himself that burnout wasn't far off if he kept grinding as he had been the last few months. Money wasn't the issue; he could use the remainder of his recent bonus to make it happen. The real question was whether Jessica would be willing to sacrifice seven days of her schedule to relax and unwind. What he didn't need was a remote work arrangement. The best thing for him was no work and all play — to relax with his woman and forget about everything and everyone, including Aris.

Luke finally nodded, accepting his friend's timely advice. "Yeah. I hear you, man."

~ 8 ~

Aris finished cleaning her space and collapsed into the hydraulic chair. She had been on her feet for twelve hours, resulting in a very profitable work day. The tips alone were enough to keep her energized despite the exhaustion she felt.

She had to check her phone more than once to even remember what day it was, which really didn't matter because it would be at least another week before she finally had a day off. As difficult as her schedule had been since Kim's accident, she refused to complain. The extra money was more than worth it.

Scrolling through her notifications, she saw that Luke hadn't called her back. She was rushing when she called him earlier, taking the one free moment she had between clients to follow up after his missed calls and messages of the past week. She could barely remember the few words she'd left on his voicemail before she hung up. There was too much to say, and she had no intention of sharing it in front of her clients so she decided to make it quick and check in with him later.

Waving goodbye to the night manager, she grabbed her bag and left the boutique. The hustle and bustle had not yet died down with women and teen girls occupying every available chair. She smiled, certain that Kim would be pleased if she were there to see the action for herself.

On her way to the parking lot, Aris decided to give Luke another call but her phone lit up on its own as she opened the door to her car.

"Yes," she answered. "I'm on my way home."

"You better be." Kim said, her tone stern. "You work too much. I told you Tanya can help share the load."

"And I told you it's not about load, it's about the money…which is rolling in pretty nicely by the way."

"As long as you're good." Kim sighed and then there was a brief pause. "So. How's Luke?"

"I don't know. I was about to call him, but now I'm talking to you."

"You don't have to be talking to me."

"I *want* to," she replied, tapping the speaker so she could talk while texting Luke. "How are you feeling?"

"Better than yesterday."

"Cool," she replied, distracted.

Hey. Let's get together soon.
Let me know when you're free.

After sending the text message, Aris sat the phone in the cup holder and tuned back into the conversation.

As Kim shared the doctor's updates, she finally started her car and drove to the local grocer before heading to Kim's house. It had become a habit she didn't care to break, especially since she still felt responsible for Kim's accident. The surgery had gone very well, but Kim was still in physical therapy three times a week. Though she missed being at work every day and coaching her cheerleading squad, Kim decided to follow the doctor's orders and take care of herself. Not that she had much choice in the matter; Aris had been no-nonsense about Kim's recovery since she'd been released from the hospital.

They hung up after Aris pulled into Kim's driveway. Using her key to enter the house, Aris found her stretched out on the sofa watching something on the *Lifetime* network.

"Remind me to bring you some movies," Aris said, placing the grocery bags on the counter.

"Chile, please. There are plenty of good movies on here, all day every day." Kim peeked over the sofa. "You get all my stuff?"

"Yes." Aris rolled her eyes. "If you can even call this food. You're gonna be as big as that head of yours if you keep up this horrible diet."

"Shut up. *Comfort* food is good for the soul."

"So are vegetables," Aris said, waving a clear bag of produce in the air.

"Says the chick who eats crap on the regular…"

She frowned at Kim. "But you ain't me though."

After putting up the food, Aris camped out on the sofa with Kim and watched the last twenty minutes of some ridiculous drama. The main character was the target of a violent crime and hospitalized for months, planning a *Kill Bill* style rampage of revenge after discovering that her husband and his mistress had orchestrated the hit and stole all of her family's money.

"That was terrible."

Kim twisted her mouth. "It was real."

"Really dumb. It almost put me in a coma." Aris stretched, noticing Kim's pensive expression. "Are you in pain? I can get your medicine —"

"No, I was just thinking about my accident."

Aris nodded, not knowing what to say.

"Tell me what happened."

Aris searched Kim's eyes, wondering if she really meant it this time. Kim had asked her for details before but when Aris began, Kim usually stopped her. She wasn't sure what made now any different, but if Kim truly wanted to know, she was ready and willing to tell her everything. "Are you sure?"

"Yeah," Kim replied with a sad smile. "I don't want to know, but I want to know...you know?" Shaking her head, she settled back against the sofa cushions. "I almost died. Like one minute I was happy and healthy and then...I almost *died*."

They sat in silence for a short while before Aris finally disclosed every detail she could remember, including her conscious state even after the paramedics arrived and how she'd flatlined in the ambulance on the way to the hospital, but one of the paramedics refused to give up on her and brought her back.

"What was his name?" Kim asked suddenly.

"The paramedic?" Aris had blocked out so much of that experience that she couldn't recall her own actions, never mind the names of all the emergency workers and hospital staff that had a hand in saving Kim's life that night. "I can't remember. I mean, I vaguely recall what he looked like but—"

"I have to thank him."

Kim had an intent look on her face. It was the expression she often displayed at work after she'd made a final decision. And much like at work, Aris was clear that there would be no chance of changing Kim's mind about this.

She watched as Kim slowly stood from the sofa. Aris stood as well, to help her, but Kim's warning look convinced Aris to sit. Minutes later, Kim returned with a large, white envelope in her hand.

"What's this?" Aris asked as she accepted it.

"It's a token of my appreciation for saving my life." Kim held her gaze. "I need you to deliver it to the paramedic."

Aris looked at her in disbelief. "How do you expect me to find him...*without a name?*"

Kim sat and grabbed Aris's hand, tears threatening to spill from her eyes. "Please. For me. Promise."

Realizing that this really meant something to Kim, Aris squeezed her hand and wiped the tear that finally slid down her friend's face. "Stop it. Your eyes are sweating." Aris swallowed hard, doing her best not to get weepy herself. "Okay. I promise."

"Thank you so much." Kim hugged Aris. "I would do it myself, but you won't let me."

"Damn right."

"So will you start looking for him today? Tomorrow is not promised."

"Seriously?" Aris sighed. "You're just gonna milk my guilt for all its worth, huh?"

Kim laughed. "I'm just sayin'."

Aris left a half hour later, wanting to go home but feeling the weight of Kim's request on her shoulders. She had to pass the hospital anyway, so she may as well make a quick stop at the ER. She was pretty sure that she'd get a quicker response to her unusual request if she asked in person rather than call and risk being placed on hold forever.

After parking in the deck, she began her walk to the elevator banks that would take her to the main entrance of the emergency room. As soon as she arrived at the first floor and stepped off, she heard sirens. She crossed the short street and continued walking, noticing two ambulances parked in front of the entrance. Off to the right, she noticed a few emergency workers casually talking and laughing among themselves, possibly on break from their duties.

"Excuse me," Aris called out, offering a nervous smile to the group as she approached. "Umm...I'm trying to find someone. A paramedic who helped my friend a few weeks ago? I don't remember his name, but I thought if I described him..." She glanced at the face of the only woman in the group, who appeared annoyed at her request. She realized how ridiculous she must sound, as if they had time to sit around and play *Guess Who?* with her until she found the paramedic she was looking for.

Embarrassed, Aris stepped back. "She—my friend was just very grateful and wanted to thank him is all, but I'll just check with the information desk. I'm sorry to bother…" In her hasty retreat, she mistakenly stepped on someone's foot. Turning her head and looking up to apologize, she caught her breath. "You."

She studied his face, recalling it from that awful night. It was him. The paramedic who saved Kim's life.

Aris read the badge that was attached to his shirt. Marcel. That sounded familiar. She blew out an audible breath, relieved that this had turned out to be a much easier search than she anticipated. "I'm sorry," she finally said, removing the white envelope from her bag. "I'm just so glad I found you. I wanted to give you this. From my friend. She sends her sincerest and heartfelt thanks for saving her life. You may not remember her, but—"

"She was the woman in the wreck on the north side. Not too far from a car dealership, right?"

Aris nodded quickly. "Yes. Kim Franklin."

"I remember you," he said, smiling down at her as his colleagues walked away to leave them alone to talk. "Both of you. I'm glad she's well."

"She is. Still in the early stages of physical therapy, but it won't be long before she's as good as new. Thank you. Thank you so much."

"And how are you?"

Aris blinked. "I'm…fine. Just, uh…trying to be there for her as much as I can. It was scary, you know?"

"I know."

Marcel's dark eyes softened, and she instantly remembered him giving her that same look after they arrived at the hospital weeks ago. Aris had been a wreck, having watched helplessly as Kim was being worked on in the back of the ambulance, stretched out with all that equipment attached to her body, on the brink of death. There had been so much going on, but Marcel had stopped to take a moment and comfort her, to explain that they were doing everything possible to save Kim.

Suddenly realizing she was standing too close, Aris took a slight step back and smiled. "Well, I didn't mean to keep you...umm, thanks again. You do amazing work and I...*we*...we are very grateful."

"You're welcome. Aris, right?"

Her eyes widened. "Yes. How'd you—"

"You told me your name in the ambulance...needed it for our records. You have an unusual name. Pretty hard to forget."

"Yeah. My parents. I was conceived in Paris. My mother dropped the 'p' and kept the rest."

"It suits you," he said. "Beautiful."

"Thank you."

They stood quietly until Aris took another step back. "I guess I'll be going now."

"I'm actually off duty at the moment," Marcel said quickly. "If you're available...why don't you join me for dinner?"

Aris looked up at him and bit her lip. He was smiling at her casually, as if he hadn't just asked her out. Honestly, all she wanted to do was get home and dive into her bed after the grueling day she had.

Then again, she *was* pretty hungry...

Her last meal had been a cinnamon roll she grabbed from the food court during her lunch break, and she had been too tired to cook at Kim's house. Besides, she hadn't had a nice dinner in weeks. Why shouldn't she take the man up on his generous offer?

Marcel's laughter interrupted her thoughts and brought her attention back to his face. He was staring at her, clearly amused by her indecision.

"Look, no pressure," he said, good-naturedly. "I'm hungry enough to do more than grab a drive-thru burger, but I didn't feel like eating alone in a restaurant. You're welcome to join me — my treat if you allow me the pleasure of your company — or we can forget I asked and go our separate ways. Your choice."

Aris grinned at him, appreciating his easy demeanor. "My choice to join you *and* pick what we eat?"

"Deal." He nodded, a smile on his face. "My car's in the south parking deck."

"Perfect, mine is too," she said as they started walking. "You can follow me to the restaurant. I'm in the mood for seafood."

~ *9* ~

Luke climbed out of his car and shut the door. His phone was buzzing again and he had quite a bit of work to finish for a client meeting in the morning, but he ignored all of it and started walking, choosing to relax his recent rule to stay away from Aris. They had been texting each other nonstop for days, so it was only a matter of time before he ended up at her door.

He heard loud music playing before he even reached the entryway. It hadn't occurred to him that she might have company or that he should have called first. He considered that for only a moment before lifting his hand to deliver three hard knocks against the wood.

The door opened a few moments later, and Luke was greeted with the strong smell of citrus. He strolled inside as she reduced the volume of the music with the remote in her hand, his eyes taking in her head scarf, tank top and cut-off shorts. "You're actually—"

"Zip it," she said, giving him a measured glance. "I already know you got something smart to say."

He grinned, wandered over to her sofa and sat without saying another word.

"For your information, I do clean up. Sometimes." She walked back into the kitchen, her nose in the air. "I am not a complete slob, sir."

"Never said you were —"

"Zip it!"

He laughed as she turned up the music. Grabbing a magazine from the coffee table, he flipped it open to a random page and settled back against the cushions. With all the banging around Aris was doing with pots and pans along with the base rattling from her stereo, actual reading was completely out of the question. He caught himself smiling and shook his head. Despite all the noise and chaos going on around him, his agitation had completely dissolved the moment he walked through her front door.

Finally tossing the magazine aside, he noticed her cell phone lighting up on the other end of the sofa. Turning his head, he yelled, "Your phone's ringing!"

He saw her head pop up through the opening above the breakfast bar. She picked up the remote and pointed it at the stereo to reduce the volume. "What?"

"Your phone's ringing."

"Who is it?"

He reached for the phone and checked the screen. "Kim."

"Answer it for me, please? My hands are icky."

The called had already dropped. He was about to tell her it went to voicemail when it began sounding off again in his hand. He swiped the screen. "Hello?"

"Well, hel-lo to you," he heard Kim reply with barely disguised delight in her voice. "*Please* tell me this is Luke Donovan answering my girl's phone."

"Hey, Kim. It's me."

"Yaaasss!"

He raised an eyebrow as he listened to her cackle.

"Just tell her to call me back later," Kim finally said. "No rush *at all*."

As Luke listened to Kim's continued laughter, he watched Aris wiggle her way over to him with a dish towel in her hand.

"Nah," he replied to Kim. "She's been cleaning her stove and…" He raised an eyebrow as she kept wiggling to the beat of the music. "Moving around…"

Aris cut her eyes at him. "I'm dancing!"

"That's what you call it?" he replied sadly, shaking his head with the phone still pressed against his ear.

"Wait," he heard Kim ask. "She's cleaning her *stove*? For what?"

That made Luke laugh. "Yeah, I wondered the same thing. Hold on."

Aris snatched the phone from him and scowled. "Hey chick…what's up?"

As she chatted with Kim on the phone, Luke went in search of the remote to the stereo. Once he found it, he grabbed a soda from the refrigerator and returned to the sofa to stretch out. After turning off the music, he scrolled through the channels looking for a game to watch but came across a reality show instead. Twenty minutes later, he was still watching it when Aris wandered back into the living room.

"You're a Primetime fan?" she asked.

"Not really."

They watched as Tracy Edmonds strutted on screen, bantering with her husband and kids. "Ah. You're a Tracy Edmonds fan." Plopping down on the sofa next to him, she nodded her head in approval. "I get it."

"Whatever," he shrugged, acknowledging to himself the head-to-toe similarities the reality star shared with Jessica. He felt her observing him, but he kept his eyes glued to the screen.

They sat in silence for the next ten minutes, enjoying the show. During a commercial break, Luke pressed a button on the remote and the television screen went black. "Wanna go watch the game?"

"Sure," she replied, turning to face him. "We can go to a different sports bar if you want. Doesn't matter to me. As long as the food is decent."

He grinned. "No sports bar tonight. Get dressed."

"Okay," she said slowly, glancing at the wall clock. "But the game doesn't start for a couple of hours. Why do we need to leave now —"

He gently placed a finger against his lips before letting his hand cover both of hers which were resting in her lap. "Just go get dressed...please?"

Narrowing her eyes, she stood from the sofa and walked away slowly before disappearing into her bedroom. Thirty minutes later, she emerged donned in an oversized Cowboys t-shirt, blue jeans and sneakers with her hair pulled up into a high, messy ponytail. Grabbing her jacket, she breezed past him on her way to the front door, leaving a flirty, cheerful scent in her wake. "Thought you were in a rush?"

Shaking his head, he led her down to his car and opened the passenger-side door. She stuck out her tongue and ducked her head to get inside, pulling the door closed before he could. When he climbed in and started the car, he felt her eyes on him but he blasted the radio and drove out of Cypress Lake in silence.

Fifteen minutes later, Aris looked at him and broke her silence. "Where are we going?"

He took his eyes off the road and glanced in her direction. "AT&T Stadium."

"Say what now?" She leaned forward to get a better view of his expression. "You're bullshittin' me...are you serious?"

"I'm serious." He eased off the highway. "Are you okay with that?"

"Shit yeah...I've never been there before." She paused at the thought and started wiggling in her seat. "Oh my God! We're actually going to the game!"

"Yes," he replied, laughing at her horrible dancing. "We're actually going to the game."

Appreciating her excitement, Luke didn't bother to explain that he'd invited her to go with him because Jessica had canceled just hours before. He'd received the tickets earlier in the week from one of his vendors, but as usual, Jessica's schedule was so air-tight that there was rarely ever an opportunity for spontaneity. Irritated, he told her he was going anyway. He refused to let the tickets go to waste and, since Devin was out of town, he thought of Aris.

She was a football fan, so it was a win-win.

After calming down and settling back against her seat, she grabbed his hand and squeezed. "I appreciate you, Luke Donovan."

He expected her to release his hand, but she held on and linked her fingers through his. It was as much a surprise to him as the casual way she had hugged him after he drove her home the first night they met. He stole a quick glance at her, but her attention was captured by the activity outside her window. Returning his gaze to the road, Luke surprised himself by not pulling his hand away. Something about the simple gesture calmed him, taking the edge off from his earlier irritation with Jessica.

As they cruised up AT&T Way and approached the stadium, Aris's mouth fell open. "It looks like a damned spaceship!"

"I'm surprised you've never even driven by here before," he replied. "Just to see it."

"I never really thought about it." She whistled. "So this is the crown jewel of the NFL? Wow."

"Wait until you actually get inside. It's sick...you'll love it. The broadcast doesn't do this place justice."

After parking in the silver lot, they hung out on the beautifully manicured lawns of the Plazas until the game started. Eventually, they wandered over to the Miller Lite Corral in the west end zone to enjoy the live music stage. With the DJ booth, bar, concession carts, and numerous televisions including the centerpiece 90-inch screen, Aris freaked. The closer they got to game time, Luke literally had to drag her away from the festivities, promising that they would come back and hang out some more after the game.

Her eyes widened. "This stays open *after* the game?"

He nodded, wrapping his arm around her shoulder.

After entering the stadium, Aris followed Luke to their seats on the lower level just to the left of the fifty-yard line. When he excused himself to take the call, she nodded absently, still in awe of the sheer size and beauty of the interior. When he returned a short while later bearing gifts — popcorn, soda and hot dogs--she started wiggling in her seat and dug into the food.

"Having fun yet?"

"Meh...just a little," she replied with a huge smile.

By the top of the second quarter, the food was gone and they were both on their feet screaming their heads off. The home team was down by three near the red zone, and the energy was electric. When the top receiver caught the pass on third down and ran it in for a touchdown, the crowd went crazy.

Luke glanced over, grinning at how into the game Aris was. Typically, he would just sit quietly in the seat and stay cool because Jessica wasn't much of a football fan and she didn't care much for all the theatrics that the game brought out of its fans.

Aris couldn't have been more different. She had been more animated and reckless than he was...

And he loved every minute of it.

When the Cowboys won at the end of the game, Aris and Luke celebrated the win with the strangers seated around them. She was screaming so loud he was sure her voice would be gone by morning. Grinning, he asked if she was ready to go back outside and she nodded eagerly, following him out of the stadium.

It was incredible to see that the Plazas were even more lively and fun than they'd been before the game thanks to the home team win. People were dancing and drinking and eating and celebrating without a care in the world.

"This is so much better than that hole in the wall sports bar I've been wasting my money on..."

"Well, we can make this a thing...if you want." Luke looked down at her and smiled. "Whenever I get home game tickets, it's me and you..."

"...and booze!" she screamed, holding up her half-empty beer in the air.

As he tapped his bottle against hers, they toasted to the big win and to their budding friendship.

~ *10* ~

"Are you ready to go?"

Jessica nodded at Luke though her expression suggested the opposite. He ignored it, placing a hand under her elbow as he guided her out of the ballroom, through the lobby and out of the hotel.

After the valet brought the car around, Luke gave him a generous tip while Jessica inserted herself into yet another conversation with one of her father's long-time associates standing a short distance away. Jessica's gaze eventually drifted to Luke, his rigid jaw prompting her to abruptly say goodnight and join him in the car. As Luke drove off the property, he felt Jessica's eyes boring a hole into the side of his face, but he kept his focus on the road.

"I'm just tired, baby," Luke explained. "Not in the mood for people tonight."

"That's obvious." She scrolled through her phone.

"I'll take care of you when we get home."

He raised an eyebrow.

She looked up and laughed. "A *massage*."

Luke seriously doubted that would be all between them, but he wasn't complaining. He was tense, having worked forty-two hours over the past three days. The only reason he wasn't working tonight was because of her father's event.

Bypassing his apartment, Luke decided to head to Jessica's place for the night. When they arrived, he followed her into the house and up the stairs, his jacket and tie yanked off before he made it to her bed. Jessica was pacing and texting, her eyes glued to her phone.

"Hey," Luke said. "Where's your laptop? I'm going to get the tickets for Savannah tonight." He glanced at his watch. "I got about a half hour before the sale fares are over."

"Why were you waiting for sale fares? It's not that much. Wait a minute...when is that for?"

"The weekend after next."

Her eyes widened. "Really? I could've sworn you said next month."

Luke watched her. "It's the weekend after next."

"I'm sorry, baby. I'm going to be in New York that weekend." She paused, noticing his jaw going rigid again. "I can't go with you to Savannah."

"I told you weeks ago."

"Luke, you know how many things I've been juggling lately...how was I supposed to remember that? I don't know why you just can't put things on our joint calendar to prevent these conflicts —"

"Because I'd rather *tell* you, which I did." Luke

crossed the room and stood over her. "Everything in life shouldn't be scheduled like a damn business appointment, Jessica. This is family."

"I know baby, and I am so sorry. But it's the only weekend we could all get together for our girls' trip." She balanced herself on her toes, kissing the corner of his mouth. "Tell your family I said hello for me, okay?"

Reaching up to stroke the side of his face, she shifted her mouth to cover his completely. He stiffened, but she deepened the kiss and pressed against him anyway. Though he instinctively responded to her advances, Luke eased out of Jessica's embrace and left her standing alone in the middle of the bedroom.

"Come on, girl...you know you like it," Marcel teased. "Open wide."

Aris cut her eyes playfully but did as he asked. A second later, she was licking her lips, savoring the flavors exploding in her mouth. "Mmm. Yummy."

"You should order it next time."

Aris ignored the question in his eyes and focused on her own meal. Marcel was a lot of fun, but she could tell he had no interest in remaining friends as she had hoped. Not that something more was out of the question. Marcel was very attractive and definitely worth a test drive, especially now that the wine was slowing revving up her dormant libido.

She watched him stand from the table and enjoyed the light brush of his finger against her cheek. "Where are you going?"

"To the restroom," he replied. "I'll be right back."

Shrugging, she twirled more pasta onto her fork. Just as she took a bite, she heard a loud buzz from her bag. She reached inside to pull out her phone, surprised to see that she'd missed four text messages. Three were sent from Ralph over an hour ago, but the most recent one was from Luke.

Smiling, she opened Luke's message. Seconds later, she replied yes to his invitation for wings and beer at the sports bar and dropped her phone into her bag just as Marcel returned to the table.

"Everything all right?"

"Yeah," she replied, picking up her fork. She twirled more pasta and took another bite. "Nothing urgent...I just have to meet a friend before I head home tonight."

"Kim?" he asked, taking a sip of wine. "How's her recovery coming along?"

"No, not Kim...but she's doing great. She's just tired of being trapped in the house."

Aris continued chatting about Kim, grateful that Marcel didn't question her further about her sudden plans after dinner. Not that she owed him anything. They weren't involved like that even though it was clearly what Marcel was hoping would happen.

For her, the jury was still out.

Their conversation flowed easily for the next hour as they ordered dessert and laughed about everything and nothing. The server circled impatiently several times but finally left them alone after Marcel placed another ten dollars in her palm before she cleared their empty dishes.

"So, Aris Collier...another great evening and I can't wait for the next." He smiled at her. "When can I see you again?"

She returned his smile, genuinely looking forward to another date with him. Placing her napkin on the table, she stood and walked over to him, placing a kiss on his cheek. "Soon enough, Mr. Baylor."

~ *11* ~

Forty minutes after Luke and Aris ordered, the food arrived at their booth. Aris was beyond annoyed at the slow service and her warm beer, grumbling about why they even bothered frequenting the place anymore. Entertained by her signature mood swings, Luke had just been teasing her about it when the server arrived.

Misinterpreting Aris's narrowed eyes and tight-mouthed expression, the server quickly asked if the food had come out to their satisfaction. Luke laughed and told the woman that the food was fine, and Aris's glare was specifically for him.

Relieved, the server relaxed into a small smile and moved on to the next booth. Luke glanced at her and noticed that she could barely keep the silly grin from splitting through the fake frown she was giving him.

"Whatever, Donovan," she replied, ignoring the satisfied smirk on his face. "I don't know why you think you know me..."

He chuckled. "Are you *not* in a funk right now?"

"Barely." She blinked. "Yes."

"Then I *do* know you." Reaching across the table, he grinned and presented his hand to her, palm up. "Give me your hand."

Matching his smile, she obliged.

After Luke blessed the food, she settled back against the back cushion of the booth and inhaled the spicy aroma of the hot wings. Though her dinner with Marcel had been excellent, she couldn't stop her mouth from watering. She couldn't believe she still had the desire and room for more.

Grabbing a small plate, she pulled six of the twenty wings from the basket along with ten celery sticks. When she finally looked up, she noticed Luke staring at her. "What?"

"Just something else we have in common," he replied. "I don't do drums either."

"Oh. Well—"

"Nah, it's cool." He grabbed a few drums from the basket. "Enjoy. I'll remember that for next time."

"Next time," Aris confirmed as she dipped a celery stick into a small, ceramic cup of ranch dressing.

Minutes passed as they ate in silence. Luke's phone buzzed several times, but he didn't bother to check the screen again after his first peek. Reaching for more celery sticks, she glanced at him and tilted her head at the sober expression settling on his face. "Looks like now we're both in a place."

He caught her eyes but remained silent.

"Com'on...you can tell me." She pushed her plate to

the side and rested both elbows on the table, her head in her hands. "What? Your woman finally giving you the blues about spending time with me?"

Raising an eyebrow, Luke simply stared at Aris.

"Oh...too soon?" Aris asked, laughing. "All right. My bad. I thought almost four whole weeks of friendship was long enough to begin talking about our significant others. Shit, you witnessed my crazy with Ralph the night we met. You may as well tell me about your woman...who I'm pretty sure exists."

Luke shook his head, smiling as he sipped his beer. "Pretty sure, huh?"

"Uh, yeah...have you seen you?" She rolled her eyes to the ceiling as if Luke ever being single was the most ridiculous concept in the world. "What's her name anyway?"

He paused. "Jessica."

"Well, it looks like Miss Jessica certainly has you bothered tonight. And you call *me* moody." Aris shook her head and offered a smile. "Ah well, I hope it all works out." Raising her mug in the air, Aris waited for Luke to join her in a toast. "To fucked-up moods."

Luke's eyes danced as they tapped their mugs.

An hour later, they were completely buzzed. After they consumed a few cups of water, Luke paid the bill and walked Aris to her car before climbing in his own and following her to Cypress Lake. On the highway, she removed her phone from her bag and called him.

"What's wrong?" Luke asked without saying hello.

"Nothing." She paused. "Wanna come over?"

"Sure. Let me drop my car, then I'll walk over."

Smiling, Aris hung up without saying goodbye.

Once they were in her living room, Luke stretched out on the sofa and stared listlessly at the ceiling. He seemed down again and, for a moment, she wondered if it was because of Miss Jessica. Dropping her bag on the floor, she disappeared into her bedroom and came out several minutes later with a video camera in her hands.

"You need cheering up, and I need help."

Watching her warily, Luke raised an eyebrow in question. "Go on..."

"First, you have to say you'll do it."

He sat up. "Do what, Moody?"

"Promise me and then I'll tell you."

Luke dropped his head and groaned before he looked up and leveled an impatient gaze on her. "Fine. I'll do it. Now *what* is it?"

"Let's make a movie!"

His eyes lazily ran the length of her body.

"Seriously?" She grabbed a pillow from the sofa and threw it at his head, rolling her eyes as he shrugged his shoulders. "I meant a *horror* movie...like we talked about. Remember when I told you I was thinking about doing one?"

"Yeah...so what?" he asked. "I'm supposed to be the cameraman or something?"

"No," she replied, smiling as she kneeled in front of him and begged him with her eyes. "I want you to be my star."

Hours later, Luke was wondering what the hell he'd gotten himself into.

But as much as he didn't care to be getting layered in makeup, he had to admit that it had completely taken his mind off of his argument with Jessica on the way back from the sports bar.

Aris had a way of relieving his stress and helping him relax without even trying. Truth be told, he could get used to this feeling.

She'd been working on him for the past hour, carefully creating the fake gashes on his forehead, neck and arms. She'd refused to let him see the process, wanting him to get the full effect of his transformation when she was done. Twenty minutes later, she stepped back to observe her work.

"You're perfect!"

"What exactly do you call yourself doing?" he asked as she started bouncing around.

"My happy dance."

He laughed. "You need a new one."

After sticking her tongue out, she rushed to her bedroom and returned with a hand mirror. "Go ahead and take a look...you look great!"

"I'll be the judge of that." He looked at her from the corner of his eye before he grabbed the mirror and peeked at his reflection. He sat up straight and looked closer. "Damn, Moody...you got skills for real." He turned at different angles to see the full scope of her work, completely impressed. Returning the mirror, he stood to his feet. "So, what's your plan for this video?"

"I'm too tired now."

He laughed out loud, shooting her an incredulous

look that translated into: *Bullshit…we're doing this.*

"I was thinking instead of the video, I can just take pictures," she said with a sheepish grin. "Now that I know you're the perfect model, we can brainstorm the details of the horror flick later and schedule the shoot for another night."

Shrugging his shoulders, he followed her around the apartment as she took different shots of him. He felt like an idiot at first as she directed his poses but after a while he started to get into it.

"If I didn't know better, I'd say you're loving this…"

He flashed the fangs she'd just forced him to put in his mouth. "You're right…you don't know better."

Just as she was about to take another picture, he felt his phone buzz against his hip. After checking the screen, he pulled the fangs from his mouth and answered the call. He listened as Jessica apologized for the tenth time about missing his family's gathering due to her scheduling mishap. When she prompted him for a response, his eyes shifted to Aris and he told Jessica they could discuss it tomorrow. He waited for her to push the issue and ask him to spend the night at her place, which she did, but he declined and said he would call her back. He was no longer in the mood to talk about it.

Hanging up, he glanced at Aris. She was busy doing something on her laptop. He asked what she was doing and she waved him over excitedly to show him the shots she'd just taken.

"That's incredible," he said, nodding in amazement. "I can't even tell that it's me."

"Thanks. I couldn't have done it without you."

She turned her head to smile at him, and his eyes dropped to her mouth. He pulled back slightly and looked away, quelling his urge to kiss her. He'd been doing that a lot tonight.

Sensing the tension between them, she hopped up from the chair and crossed the room. "I know you have to go, but you can't go like that." She left the room and returned with more stuff. "Let me fix you."

A half hour later, Luke was himself again. Aris walked him out, making him promise to brainstorm ideas for her horror flick the next time he came over to which he agreed. After she closed and locked the door, he sprinted toward his building...already missing her before he made it into his apartment.

~ 12 ~

The day came and went, but Luke never saw Jessica.

Around noon, she called to explain that she was stuck in an impromptu, off-site meeting so their lunch date was canceled. Around 3PM, she text him saying that she was expecting a client at 4PM and was planning to take him and his wife to dinner later that evening. When she asked that he join them at the restaurant, he declined and drove to his apartment.

Once he pulled into his driveway, he called Aris.

Unfortunately, she was working late too.

Unable to shake his irritation, he decided to go for a run around the neighborhood. He had hoped that it would clear his head, but all it did was give him too much quiet time to think about Aris.

Thoughts of her were starting to become his default.

Several miles later, Luke circled back to his building, entered his apartment and took a long shower. When he returned to his bedroom, he noticed the flashing light on his phone. Probably a missed call and message from Jessica insisting that he join her for dinner. She could give a damn about putting him off all day when they really needed to talk, but now she needed to see him to handle some business? Whatever. He hadn't made her top-five-important-things-to-do list today, so fuck a client dinner. Why should he give a damn how his absence appeared when she could not care less about how it was going to look when he flew to Georgia to see his family without her...again?

Snatching his phone from the nightstand, he entered his code and checked his notifications. There were two missed calls from Jessica...and a text from Aris.

Wanna come over?

He was dressed in seconds and knocking on her door five minutes later. When she opened the door, he almost choked...and then he laughed.

"Don't ask," she said, laughing with him. "Come on in. I'd offer you some food but as you can see by all the smoke, I kinda burned it all up."

Settling on the sofa, Luke watched as she walked over to open the patio door to allow the smoke to drift out. Then, she dug through her hall closet and pulled out an oscillating fan which she plugged into the wall and aimed toward the open windows.

Satisfied, she turned to him and shrugged. "I could order pizza or something."

Before he could respond, she was already calling to place an order. Hanging up, she crashed onto the sofa next to him and passed him one of the two bottles of beer she grabbed from the kitchen before she placed her bare feet on the edge of the coffee table. Seconds later, she released a long, high-pitched sigh.

"Bad day?"

"Dude...you have no idea. Sucked so bad that me almost burning down this apartment building doesn't even rank in the top five bad things of the day." She grabbed the remote and passed it to him. "But at least it's all behind me. How about you? Given how lousy my day was, yours should have been awesome."

"You think so, huh?"

"Had to be. It would mess up the natural order of things if it wasn't." She sipped her beer. "Balance."

"Well, I hate to disappoint you but as far as me having an awesome day? Not so much."

"Damn," she replied, shaking her head.

Leaning back against the sofa cushions, Luke opened his arms and waited until Aris settled against him. "Yep," he said. "The universe sucks."

"No, that's not possible. The universe is the universe. So the only thing that makes sense is that *we* suck," she said, taking back the remote from him and scrolling through the channel menu.

"Okay...then, I guess all we can do is try to suck less tomorrow," he said, tapping his bottle with hers.

"To sucking less. I like it." She took a swig. "We should totally start a support group."

He nodded. "Just me and you."

"And booze."

Aris finally settled on a football game which pleased Luke more than he cared to admit. After the pizza arrived, they ate in comfortable silence and enjoyed the game until they were full. Luke opened his arms again and they returned to their earlier lounging position with Aris curled up next to him.

He heard her soft snores about a half hour later.

Closing his eyes, he finally allowing himself to really enjoy the feeling of being so close to her. She fit perfectly in his arms, and her tangled mess of hair was a lot softer than he expected it to be...just like her skin as he caressed her arms. Unable to stop himself, he pressed his lips to her temple, over and over, until he felt her begin to stir. He hadn't meant to wake her, but now that she was up...

She lifted her head to look at him and his chest tightened. He expected her to sit up, to move away... but she did neither. She just kept staring.

"You're so pretty." His eyes swept her face, a hint of a smile forming on his lips. "So pretty..."

Leaning in slowly, he finally kissed her and heard her gasp as he pulled her bottom lip into his mouth, felt her shudder when he traced his tongue over the soft flesh...

"Luke...wait."

Dizzy, he ignored her and continued nipping at her lips, enjoying the moans and sighs escaping them as she eventually stopped trying to talk and kissed him back. He let his hands trail down her spine to her ass, making her gasp again before she jerked her mouth away, freeing him to kiss other areas.

"Luke, you can't," she said, panting. "Jessica."

At the sound of the truth, he reluctantly tore his mouth away from her ear and dropped his head onto her shoulder as he tried to calm his own breathing... but that only brought him closer to her scent, which compelled him to kiss the sweet spot at the curve of her neck, where he slowly ran his tongue over her skin, tasting her.

"Luke..."

He smiled at the quiver in her voice, loving the way she said his name so much that he buried his hands in her hair and shifted his mouth back to her lips...until she pulled away again. Finally opening his eyes, he could see the confusion in hers along with something else he couldn't quite place.

"I can't." She paused. "I'm seeing somebody now."

Coming out of his daze, it took him a while to process her words. Once he understood, he blinked. "Ralph," he replied sarcastically, shaking his head. She moved back even further as he sat up and placed his feet on the floor. "Did you get your car back too?"

"No," Aris replied, looking away. "It's not...I'm seeing someone else. His name is Marcel."

Still staring at her, he felt his phone buzz against his hip. He knew without checking the screen that it was Jessica calling...and her timing couldn't have been more perfect. "I gotta go." He pulled on his shoes and stood, not bothering to even look in Aris's direction as he walked away.

"Luke—"

"Lock the door," he said before slamming it on his way out.

Aris sat quietly long after Luke left, unable to forget the look on his face when she told him she was seeing Marcel. His expression had been hard to interpret; however, it somehow seemed familiar and she couldn't help feeling like she did the night they first met—confused and unable to determine that if the look was one of interest or one of judgment.

After locking her door, she debated whether or not to give him a moment and then call him and talk it through. After what had just happened between them, something needed to be said...but what? Releasing a heavy sigh, she turned her attention to the stack of mail she'd left on the hallway table. She'd been in such a funk from her day that she didn't even bother to look at any of it. Probably just a bunch of overdue bills she didn't have money to pay. Needing a distraction, she walked over to the table and began sorting.

Not calling Luke was probably for the best.

Though she knew he was surprised to learn about Marcel, it was clear that wasn't his main issue. She could sense when he walked through her door earlier that he was troubled. She'd done her best to tune out his phone conversation, but the edge she heard in his voice was pretty hard to ignore. Whoever this Jessica person was, it was apparent that Luke's relationship with her was serious enough that a phone call had the power to shift him away from Aris instantly.

Not that she was really tripping over that because they were just friends. She had no intention of being anything less than completely supportive of Luke's relationship with Jessica. Besides, she didn't have time to be in their business when she was trying to figure out what she was going to do about her own situation. She'd already sort of agreed to give Marcel a real shot earlier today when she met him for lunch. It was their sixth date, and he had immediately asked to see her again right after they kissed.

But Marcel hadn't kissed her like Luke had...

Aris ran her fingers over her lips, allowing herself a few moments to dwell on the smell of him, the taste of him, the way his hands...

Shaking her head quickly, she stomped into the kitchen and poured herself a glass of lemonade though what she really needed was a double shot of bourbon. Something to take the edge off...to calm the desire that Luke had sparked within her from just one kiss...

"Stop it, Aris," she said aloud to herself after taking a big gulp. "Stop it *right now*."

Setting the glass on the counter, she returned to the hallway table. When she finally read the label of the largest envelope, she gasped and rushed over to the sofa. Her hand began shaking so badly that she dropped the rest of the letters and junk mail around it, gripping the envelope so hard that her nails almost ripped through the paper.

It was from Cinema Makeup Design Institute, one of the top makeup training schools in the country.

More specifically, Aris's *top* choice...period.

At the thought of what it could be—what it could mean—Aris tossed the envelope onto the coffee table and backed away, watching closely as if it would self-destruct. She didn't want to open it...she couldn't. If this letter said what she hoped it would, then the other responses she was waiting for from other schools didn't matter. Applying to CMDI was her Hail Mary, her one and only chance to heave the ball downfield into the open hands of the Admissions Office in a last-ditch effort to put points on the board of life and live her dreams...

Her chance to *win*.

If CMDI said yes to her, every other acceptance or denial would simply be white noise.

If they said yes.

Aris returned to the kitchen, slowly refilled her glass of lemonade, then frantically searched the cabinet for some enhancements and found a nearly-empty bottle of Vodka, pouring every ounce of its contents into the glass before taking a big, animated gulp.

Her eyes drifted to the envelope.

She couldn't do this by herself.

Glancing at the clock, Aris admitted that she didn't feel like driving all the way over to Kim's house for this. She was probably asleep already and there was no sense in waking her even though Kim was the only other person in the world who knew how much the contents of the white envelope meant to her.

Still unable to calm her shaky hands, she took another big gulp of liquid courage before racing into her bedroom. She yanked open her nightstand drawer and spread the contents of the worn, bright yellow folder over the bedspread to consume the courage she really needed...

I am truly exceptional.

I have a great voice.

I have an unusual and beautiful name.

...until finally, she came across the one strip of paper she'd been searching for:

I have a cool and unique talent.

Aris smiled as her stress began to subside.

Luke had told her that.

She wondered if he even remembered saying that to her. Probably not, but it didn't matter.

Lifting her head, she caught her reflection in the dresser mirror, a look of determination lighting her eyes. She would simply remind Luke of his words to her. Then, she would demand a temporary suspension of this...*awkwardness* between them and force him to support her — to open the envelope and reveal her fate.

After stuffing the yellow folder back into her nightstand drawer, Aris rushed back to the coffee table and grabbed the white envelope. She felt her heart racing in her chest as she considered the possibilities... and how she would react. Uncertain, she pressed her lips together. Could she trust Luke with her reaction — good or bad? He'd already seen her nut up in a public parking lot and decided to stick around. Surely, he could handle her when she collapsed into a pool of sobs if she wasn't accepted to her dream school.

Shit, that's what friends were for...

Feeling more secure, Aris grabbed her keys and walked out. It wasn't until she was standing in her driveway that she realized her phone was still in her apartment but, instead of going back for it, she kept walking. In the time it would take to go back for it to text Luke that she was on her way over, she could already be standing at his front door, knocking...so what was the point?

Pressing on, she'd almost made it across the grassy knoll that separated their buildings when her brisk walk suddenly came to a halt. Turned out that texting before showing up unannounced would have been best because he was currently busy playing tongue hockey with whom she could only assume was Jessica.

Luke had her pressed against an unfamiliar luxury car, her mini-dress hiked up with one of her spiked-heeled legs wrapped around his waist. Even from this distance, the brightness from the neighborhood light posts allowed her to clearly see that Jessica was beyond beautiful...just as she had presumed Luke's woman would be.

Suddenly realizing that she was being creepy by standing there and watching them suck each other's faces off, Aris turned abruptly and rushed back toward her apartment. Not that either one of them actually saw her, given how *involved* they both were...

As she walked into her apartment, the petty part of Aris nudged at her ego, once again alluding to her subconscious belief that a guy like Luke couldn't possibly want her. She had known that fact when she met him, so she hadn't ever allowed herself to believe otherwise. Especially since he was obviously in love with another woman...a *gorgeous* woman who was practically Tracy Edmond's freaking doppleganger.

"Had you really expected anything less?" she mumbled to herself after locking the door. Shaking off surprising stirrings of irritation, she reminded herself that Luke was her friend…

A friend who had used her.

She frowned slightly before forcefully shaking the assumption from her head, dismissing the random thought before it could set up shop in her mind.

She didn't want to believe that. She couldn't.

Luke just didn't seem like the type.

Not to mention she had welcomed him into her apartment a few times already and never once had he crossed the line in any way before tonight.

No, he was not that guy.

And though she'd actually felt something when she was in his arms earlier, it was obvious that the kiss meant nothing at all. Just a troubled man trying to ease his frustration. It had been a slip, a simple mistake on both their parts…

And one she was certain would never happen again.

Aris leaned back against her front door, twisting the envelope in her hands. Cursing, she finally ripped it open…and smiled.

She got in.

She was *accepted*.

The joyous, squealy-scream that escaped her mouth was so ridiculous that Aris collapsed on her sofa in giggles. When she calmed down, her eyes drifted about the room before she eventually marched over to the corner to pull out two of her mannequin heads.

"I did it!" she sang into their grotesque faces. "I did it! I did it! I'm in…*I'M IN!!!*"

With one head in each hand, Aris twirled and danced around her living room to the music in her head until the euphoria subsided and she eventually collapsed on her sofa. Stretching out, she laughed again—long and loud and hard—before closing her eyes and drifting into a deep, peaceful sleep.

~ 13 ~

OCTOBER

Hand-in-hand, Luke and Jessica strolled out of the community clubhouse and followed the cobblestone path leading to the swimming pool. The grounds were immaculate, complete with lush foliage and colorful plants. There were more adults than children present, and everyone was engaged in conversation or enjoying a moment of relaxation as they nibbled on the finger foods and fresh deli items being served by the Cypress Lake staff. It was a fitting welcome for new renters and a convenient opportunity for long-time residents to reconnect.

As Jessica stopped to receive a flute of champagne from one of the servers, Luke scanned the crowd until his eyes stopped at the shadiest area of the property where he found Aris curled up on a Spartan Daybed with what appeared to be a book in her hands.

"Do you want one, baby?"

Luke turned to see Jessica pointing to a platter of Hawaiian BBQ seafood skewers.

"Sure." Luke accepted one from the server, taking a bite and nodding at him in appreciation. "Thanks, man…these are good."

As Jessica inquired about the recipe, Luke excused himself to claim a couple of chairs at an empty table. He looked up and noticed Jessica and the server were now surrounded by a few other people and in deep conversation, so he sat down and waited for her to join him. Luke did his best to focus on a group of teens playing volleyball in the pool, but it wasn't long before his eyes found Aris again.

They hadn't spoken to each other since the kiss at her apartment over a week ago. After slamming Aris's door, he stood right outside her entryway and answered Jessica's second call, only to get into an argument and abruptly cut her off before hanging up the phone, irritated that she was still questioning why he refused to show up for that damn client dinner though she had yet to see an issue with choosing a getaway with her girlfriends over a trip with him to spend time with his family…but what really had him on edge was Aris's confession that she was seeing some dude named *Marcel*.

When the hell had she met him?

Luke had practically been around for the better part of a month, so either Marcel had been a factor before Luke came on the scene or Aris had picked him up right after.

As she started walking, that latter thought irritated

him more than he cared to admit. To think that Aris was *that* chick—inviting random dudes to her apartment for breakfast and shit, texting and teasing for her own entertainment—both saddened him and pissed him off.

And the idea that Marcel had probably already been to her apartment too? Possibly in her bed?

Fuck that.

During the entire walk back to his apartment, Luke had been so busy getting himself all worked up over his assumptions about Aris that he didn't even notice Jessica's car parked in his driveway. She was sitting inside the car with the door open, leaning out with her head turned his way as she watched him approach. He hadn't even waited until she turned off the ignition before he pulled her out, slammed the door and pinned her against it. Though she appeared slightly confused given they'd just been at each other's throats, she hadn't resisted him and, instead, spread her legs wide to bring him closer to her heat, giving as good as she got. Luke hadn't cared at all that they were outside underneath brightly-lit lamp posts; all he had cared about was completely deleting the kiss between him and Aris from his memory...

But not even publicly molesting and tonguing the shit out of Jessica for almost five minutes could erase what Aris tasted like, what she sounded like...how good she'd felt pressed against him and how intoxicating it was being so close to her...

Frustrated, Luke had pulled away and looked at his woman. Jessica had stared back at him, as if she wanted to question his erratic behavior, but she didn't.

Instead, she smiled knowingly…assuming she had him right where she wanted him. In that moment, she'd shifted into "fix-it" mode, ready to do whatever was sexually necessary to satisfy him and get things back in line. But as Luke followed her into his apartment and into his bed, he realized that, for the first time in their eight-year relationship, Jessica's seductive prowess would not be able to fix it this time…to fix them.

When he finally wrapped his arms around her, quietly relaxing after having sexed off and on for almost an hour, Luke was disgusted with himself because all that energy had nothing to do with Jessica.

He had been thinking of Aris.

"Baby, I'm going to go get us some of those ice cream cones," Jessica said, redirecting Luke's attention from of his shameful memory and back into the present. "They look yummy! I'll be right back."

He watched as she sauntered toward the miniature ice cream stand. Without fail, Jessica was instantly pulled into another conversation and he could immediately tell that after only a few minutes everyone in the vicinity instantly fell in love with her.

A small smile settled on Luke's face. That was his Jessica. She had been raised in the art of wooing a crowd. Her ability to connect with people was one of the things that made her father most proud. As a rising executive, Mr. Knox was grooming his daughter to expand his empire and Luke had learned a lot from them both.

Minutes later, Jessica joined him at the table to enjoy their elaborately-decorated desserts but it wasn't long before her phone buzzed. In true form, she checked the screen, gave him a quick kiss and excused herself to put out what could only be another fire because no one at Knox Corp seemed to care that it was a *Saturday* afternoon.

Concentrating on his ice cream cone, Luke nodded as she walked away. He was accustomed to her hectic schedule because he unfortunately had a similar one. The difference was he'd decided to turn his phone off so they could have an uninterrupted day.

So much for that.

Before he could stop himself, Luke's eyes traveled back to where Aris had been tucked away a short while ago but disappointment seized him as he realized she was gone.

Shaking off the disappointment, Luke waited for Jessica to return and they lounged around the pool for another hour, chatting off and on with old and new neighbors. Luke was never as comfortable as Jessica with the schmoozing, but he knew, like with all things, practice made perfect. Normally, he was the guy who preferred to fall back and observe, but that natural passiveness no longer had a place in his future so he sucked it up and turned on the charm, especially since Jessica seemed to be enjoying herself. The least he could do was act like he was too.

But after another half hour of it, he was done.

With people, with everything.

Even after they left the clubhouse and arrived at the movie theater, Luke was still distracted and slightly agitated. He'd been struggling to keep his mind off Aris, which was the reason he agreed to see a movie so he could focus his mind on something...anything...but his cute and quirky neighbor. As usual, Jessica insisted on some silly ass romantic comedy until he caved to her wishes...

But damned if the gorgeous but goofy leading lady didn't remind him of the woman he was so desperately trying to—and seriously *needed* to—forget.

Aris took a deep breath before opening her door.

As she stepped aside, Ralph entered her apartment and looked around dramatically while shamelessly inspecting her place. Careful not to roll her eyes, Aris closed the door behind him and forced a tight smile right before his gaze finally settled on her face.

She hadn't been terribly surprised when she saw Ralph's number flash across her phone's screen. The end of the month was approaching and so was her rent payment. Though she knew she couldn't afford it, Ralph had been the one to convince her to make Cypress Lake her home. She had originally protested when he bypassed the other complexes on her list to visit and drove her to Frisco to see the secluded property with its luxurious apartments and natural surroundings. Despite her objections, Aris had fallen in love with the space as they strolled through the model apartment, so much that she found herself blindly accepting Ralph's offer to cover her rent until she was able to make the payments on her own without his financial support.

That day of independence still hadn't quite come...

Which was why Ralph was now standing inside her apartment with a slick grin on his face. He wanted to remind her of that fact.

He was nothing if not a creature of habit.

Aris had let his calls roll to voicemail to send a message that her days of needing him were over. With the extra hours she'd been working at the boutique since Kim's accident, she would be able to cover her rent and much more for the next month. When his calls stopped, Aris assumed that her silent message of independence had been received until she heard incessant knocking on her door fifteen minutes later. Ralph had to know that letting his call roll over to voicemail had not been a mistake on her part, but it was just like him to not back down until he was acknowledged.

"What are you doing here, Ralph?"

Though her words were clipped and the answer was obvious, Aris managed to maintain a fairly pleasant tone, as if his showing up unannounced was not the disrespectful violation that it truly was. They stared at each other for several long moments, but Aris refused to let her eyes waver so he would know for certain that she had no intention of allowing him to have his way with her again, in any way, ever again.

"I was in the neighborhood," Ralph replied, stepping closer. "I missed your face, and I needed to see you."

She dodged his hand as he attempted to touch what he claimed to miss so much. Though he instantly stiffened at her rejection, he recovered quickly and smiled at her anyway. "How have you been?"

It was a loaded question, delivered in Ralph's terse

but casual way in a poor attempt to disguise what he really wanted to know—which was basically every minute detail of her existence and whereabouts since she hadn't been under his thumb. Aris considered telling him that she'd moved on but decided that he didn't deserve the energy it would take for her to craft a false story, so she settled on the truth. "I've been great, actually. I got an acceptance letter for school, so I'll be moving soon. CMDI wants me...they said yes."

She waited for a reaction, bracing herself for his characteristic badgering about the what, when, where, how and why of this new development. She was ready for that, for all of his mind games, but what she wasn't expecting was his humility.

"That's incredible news, sweetheart. It's what you've always wanted. Congratulations.... but it breaks my heart to know that I wasn't there to celebrate that moment with you." Keeping his hands to himself this time, Ralph moved toward her again as he gazed at her with unabashed affection. "I don't ever want to miss another important moment in your life. I want us again...but better. I want us to try, I'll try... harder than I ever have. I'll change. I'll do better. I'll support school, your art, all of it. Whatever I have to do...as long as you're with me."

For a moment, Aris let his words hang in the air, not wanting to accept them because, in the end, they never held their meaning nor maintained their worth. Noticing her indifference, Ralph kept talking, telling her to take all the time she needed, assuring her that he was sincere, that they deserved another chance and that they were meant to be together.

All Aris wanted to hear was the sound of the door closing behind him on his way out.

"Is there still a chance for us?" Ralph asked, his voice tinged with the desperation she had grown to loathe.

She opened her mouth, ready to ask him to leave her home, to leave her life for good...but a sudden knock on her front door ruined the opportunity. Frustrated by the interruption, Aris yanked the door open to find Luke on the other side of the frame. Her face lit up.

"Hey," Luke said after glancing over Aris's head at Ralph standing behind her. "What's up? Did I catch you at a bad time?"

"Uh, no," she replied, both surprised and pleased by his presence. "Not at all." She could feel Ralph's resolve fading fast, so she opened the door wider to allow Luke to enter. "Luke, this is Ralph. Ralph...this is my friend, Luke."

It was all she could do not to laugh at Ralph's expression at not being introduced as anything more than his given name. But that's all he was to her now — not her man, not her friend...just Ralph. Turning away from him, Aris smiled up at Luke. "Ralph was just leaving."

Given the obvious tension in the room, Aris wasn't surprised when Luke bypassed the verbal pleasantries and simply nodded his head in Ralph's direction in greeting. When Ralph began subtly sizing him up, Luke cocked a brow in acknowledgment prompting Ralph to smirk in response.

"Don't worry about your rent this month...I got it." Stepping forward, Ralph grabbed a clueless Aris by the waist and placed a kiss on her closed mouth before releasing her and strolling out, tossing a promising "see you later, sweetheart," over his shoulder before he slammed the door behind him.

The entire exchange lasted no more than several seconds but, by the time Aris's shock wore off, the damage had been done. Her first thought was to chase after Ralph and curse his ass out. Instead, she shook her head in disbelief and rushed to lock the door. When she turned to face Luke, she paused at his stony expression and the rigid set of his jaw. Misinterpreting his emotions as concern for her having been blindsided by Ralph, she placed a hand on Luke's arm and released a long, frustrated breath. "I know, right? I can't believe the nerve of his arrogant ass either. I'm so glad you showed up before I had to hurt his damn feelings...again. It wouldn't have been pretty."

Aris reached for Luke's hand and squeezed it gently before pulling him with her to the sofa. When he refused to sit, she gave him a confused look before she shrugged it off and launched into mindless chatter, moving about the room until she stopped to pull her chess board from the bottom shelf of the coffee table.

"I don't play games," Luke snapped.

The nastiness of his tone caught her off guard, but she looked up and smiled at him anyway. "You don't play or you don't know how to play?"

Her eyes knitted at the look of disgust settling across his face, so she decided that maybe he just needed time to cool off before he was ready to tell her what was really wrong with him. She proceeded to set up the pieces on the board, all the while assuming that the only reason Luke was still standing up looking like he was ready to rip someone's head off was because his supermodel girlfriend had pissed him off yet again.

Aris had seen them at the community event earlier and, from her distant view, they seemed like the quintessential happy couple out on a sunny Saturday afternoon. As much as she had tried to keep her eyes focused on her book, Aris couldn't help but observe them—observe Jessica—and how disturbingly perfect the two of them looked together.

Before long, her peace evaporated and left her with feelings she didn't care to own. She gathered her things and moved slowly through the crowd toward the side exit, the pettiest part of her wondering if Luke would bother to stop her hasty retreat and say hello or if maybe he would introduce her to Jessica as his friend. But the closer she got to the exit, the more she realized that he probably hadn't even seen her, let alone searched for her in the dense crowd of neighbors.

The fact that she was so bothered by this surprised Aris, but she refused to admit that it mattered.

Even now, with him standing here, she refused to acknowledge the disturbing flutter deep in the pit of her stomach, all because he decided to come see her.

None of it mattered...because they were just friends.

Despite his nasty attitude and the unfriendly scowl he was currently directing her way.

To lighten the mood, Aris decided now was as good a time as any to share her amazing news. "Hey! Guess what? Remember I told you about all those schools I'd applied to?" Not waiting for his reply, she released a little squeal of excitement and started wiggling. "Well, I got accepted...to Cinema Makeup Design Institute! It was my top choice!"

"Wow." Luke blinked, a genuine smile slowly breaking through his foul mood. "That is great news. I'm happy for—"

"And...I'll be moving to Los Angeles!"

As Aris began twirling in glee, Luke's smile instantly faded. "Wait...you what?"

"I'm moving to L.A.," she said again, stopping her spins. When she noticed the irritated expression on his face, she tilted her head and moved closer. "CMDI is in Los Angeles, and I'm leaving in December to start class in January. That's what I was telling Ralph right before you showed up but as usual he used it as an opportunity to reinsert himself into the equation because he didn't want to lose me and yada, yada, yada. Can you believe him?" She shook her head again and laughed. "First, he shows up here unannounced and then he acts like I wasn't completely serious when I told him it was absolutely over between us—"

"Oh that's right," Luke said, cutting her off and releasing a humorless laugh. "Because now you're with *Marcel*."

Narrowing her eyes, she backed away slowly and placed her hands on her hips. "All right, you've been nasty and borderline mean to me the entire time you've been here...so what's this really about? You and Jessica at each other's throats again and I'm an easy target for your fucked-up attitude?"

"Jessica and I are just fine. The only person she's kissing and fucking is me, so I couldn't be better."

Her nostrils flared as she took a deep breath. Turning on her heel, she left him standing in the living room and walked into the kitchen. "Would you like some water, juice or something?"

"Nah. I'm not staying long."

"So what was the point of you coming by?" Aris finally snapped, slamming a glass on the counter. "To kiss me until who you really want starts acting right?"

Luke twisted his mouth and shook his head before he crossed the room and yanked her front door open.

Running her hands over her hair, Aris closed her eyes and sighed. "Luke, just…wait. I shouldn't have said that. I'm…look, I don't want to do this with you."

He looked over his shoulder and gave her a frosty look. "Me neither. Not at all."

"Will you stop? Just stop…and *talk* to me, all right? What's going on with you today? Things seemed fine earlier when I saw you and Jessica at the clubhouse, but now you're standing there ready to rip somebody's head off…shit, rip *my* damn head off."

When Luke turned around, Aris waited for him to explain. Instead, he remained silent.

"What happened, Luke? Have you even tried talking to her about it or have you just been brooding all day long? If you need to vent, I'm listening. But you have to *talk* to me, not attack me." Crossing the room, she reached out and grabbed his hand. He looked away. "Look at me. I know something is rattling you…what is it?" She paused, observing him. "Is it her father?"

His finally looked at her, surprise in his eyes.

"You seemed so irritated that day in my apartment when you took that call out on the patio…were you talking to him then?" she asked, probing further. "And the few times you've talked to me about Jessica, you always sound so...I don't know. Disconnected or something. I get that she's the trophy, but you don't seem okay to me." Aris searched his face for a sign of understanding as her own past issues with Ralph began surface in her mind. "Are you happy? Or does it sometimes just feel like she's more trouble than she's worth—?"

"Like you?"

She turned away, stepping back like she'd been hit.

"No. *She's* actually worth it. You on the other hand are nothing more than an attention whore stringing dudes along for entertainment." He hesitated when she flinched but, a moment later, his words tumbled out again. "I'm curious though...how many of us is it?"

Wrapping her arms around her body, she kept her back to him. "That's what you think...that I'm stringing you along?"

"Oh shit, you know what? You're right...I'm not exactly included in the count because I'm just one of your *friends.*"

"Friends?" she asked before taking a seat on the edge of the sofa and placing her head in her hands. "I actually thought we were...until now."

"It doesn't matter. I got enough friends." He stood in the doorway and tossed one last look over his shoulder. "Good luck, Hollywood. It's been real."

After the door slammed, Aris sat quietly as Luke's words swirled around in the air until they grabbed hold of her, seeping into her soul. Still perched on the edge of the sofa, she stayed that way until her cell phone buzzed and she looked over to see Marcel's face flashing across the screen.

Letting it roll to voicemail, she ignored the stinging in her eyes and rose from the sofa. After locking the door, she moved to the darkest corner of the living room and pulled out her tools to begin working on her latest mannequin...

Like nothing ever happened.

~ 14 ~

After securing his seatbelt, Luke flagged a frail flight attendant to order something to take his edge off. To avoid eye contact with the boarding passengers, he turned his head to stare through the tiny window until his drink arrived.

The faint reflection staring back at him was yet another reminder that he looked like shit. It had been days since he'd gotten a good night's sleep. What should have been a relaxing vacation resulted in remote work in an exotic location.

Though he and Jessica still managed to enjoy themselves in between dozens of business calls and virtual meetings, Luke was pissed. Here he was calling himself stepping up and whisking his woman away on a romantic, extended weekend getaway, but they barely did more than sync their upcoming schedules when they weren't syncing their bodies. Not that he was complaining about the sex because Jessica had pulled out all the stops and kept him drained, but what he'd really needed from her was *intimacy*.

Unfortunately, the night he planned to express that specific need to her was the same night her father called and insisted they return stateside for a Monday night event with a key client. Luke watched in silence as Jessica excused herself from the table and left him to finish eating alone in the center of the restaurant. When she returned with her phone still stuck to her ear thirty minutes later, Luke had already generously tipped the server. He ignored Jessica's protests that she hadn't finished her food and placed her packaged entrée in her hands before escorting her back to their suite.

An apology of some sort was a given considering all the trouble he'd gone through to make their evening so special...or so he thought because the apology never came. Instead, Jessica continued yapping on the phone while he drove. As soon as they entered their suite, she pulled out her tablet and searched departure times, ready to change their Tuesday afternoon return flights to early Monday so they could meet her father in New York. Enjoying the final day of their so-called vacation was the furthest thing from her mind.

Luke still couldn't remember what words came out of his mouth after he snatched the tablet out of her hands but, needless to say, he remained in Puerto Vallarta Monday morning and Jessica caught the six thirty-five a.m. flight to New York alone.

"A Crown and Coke for the gentleman."

"Thank you," Luke replied to the flight attendant after accepting his drink.

"May I assist you with anything else…sir?"

Her offer was so obvious that all Luke could do was chuckle. Here this woman was throwing her pussy at him, but *his* woman always had better places to be than by his side. Though pitifully humorous to him, Luke regretted his outward display of amusement as soon as he saw the flight attendant's sweet smile disappear.

"Forgive me." He shook his head, returning her offer with an apologetic smile. "Life is just funny sometimes. I appreciate you, but I'm good."

The woman's smile returned as she blatantly glanced at his bare ring finger and shook her head. "Doesn't she know it's not safe to leave you by yourself?"

He chuckled again, glad that the woman had a sense of humor. "I guess not."

"Shame, shame." She winked. "Enjoy your flight."

After takeoff a short while later, he did everything but enjoy the turbulent ride. With the bad weather and the obnoxious kid wreaking havoc behind his seat, Luke wondered if this was karma for the fight he'd had with Jessica just hours before she boarded her flight for New York.

He hadn't spoken to her since.

Exiting the plane and walking through the terminal, Luke considered calling Jessica to let her know he landed but he decided to deal with her later. He had no idea if she was at her house, in the office or still in New York…and he had no intention of going anywhere else but his apartment.

An hour later, he was sitting on the edge of his bed, glad to be home but already missing the ocean breeze and freedom he'd left behind. Releasing a long, travel-weary breath, he fell back against the comforter and looked up to catch the hypnotic spin of the ceiling fan.

He needed to see Aris.

Luke cringed as he recalled their last interaction. He hadn't meant what he said to her. He was just being a dick, unable to deal with the depth of feelings he was beginning to have for her. It didn't help matters when her ex kissed Aris right in front of him to prove a point like she was nothing more than a piece of property of some shit. It was all Luke could do not to ram his fist in dude's face for such disrespect. The level of anger he'd felt in that moment shocked and agitated him even more until Aris finally set him off by casually tossing out that she was moving to California of all places… over a thousand miles away from him…

Luke sat up and cursed his reflection as he stared into the dresser mirror at the foot of his bed.

He didn't want Aris to leave.

From the moment he saw Ralph standing in her apartment with that satisfied look on his face, the possibilities unnerved him. He'd been jealous even after Ralph left, completely pissed off and taking his frustration out on Aris…

Because she fucking *mattered* to him.

Cursing again, Luke rushed into the bathroom to take a shower. After throwing on clothes, he left his apartment, jogged over to Aris's building and climbed the stairs two at a time until he was standing at her front door.

Raising his hand to knock, he paused. He had been so focused on seeing and apologizing to her that he hadn't bothered to consider that she might be alone.

"Fuck that," he mumbled to himself as he delivered a series of hard knocks to her front door.

A few seconds passed. No answer.

He checked the time on his phone and cursed again. It was Wednesday. He had no idea if she worked on Wednesdays...hell, he'd never thought to ask her about her work schedule before—

The door flew open.

Aris stood barefoot in a tee and some cotton shorts, her face expressionless as she stared at him silently.

Luke released the first real smile he'd had all day.

He watched as she flashed him a look of annoyance before she turned and disappeared into her apartment. It was obvious that she was less than thrilled to see him...but she left the door open.

Taking that as a positive sign, he stepped inside her apartment and locked the door behind him. As he entered the living room, he noticed Aris sitting in a rotating desk chair facing her flat panel television. Crossing the room, Luke stopped to stand between her and the cable receiver just as she was about to press play on the remote control.

"Aris...I'm sorry for what I said. For labeling you. It was low...and disrespectful. I guess that kiss between us fucked me up a little bit...a lot, actually. Then Marcel came on the scene...and then days later I see Ralph all in your space like..." He ran a hand over his head a few times before he dropped both arms to his sides. "I'm sorry. It was a lot and I reacted without thinking, but that's no excuse. I had no right. I never should've said those things to you. We're friends and I crossed the line...and it will never happen again."

He stepped closer, forcing her to look up at him.

She stared quietly, her expression unchanged.

He couldn't read her at all.

Is she mad? Is she over it?

A slight panic filled his chest.

Is she over us?

Luke shook his head, surprised at how desperate he actually felt at the mere thought that this girl might not ever speak to him again. She continued to stare at him, and he waited for something...anything.

He was anxious as hell.

When the fuck had *that* started happening?

Dropping to his knees in front of her, Luke reached up to brush a wayward strand of hair from her face. "By the way, I think it's great that you got accepted to your top school. I'm sorry that I didn't actually say that to you right after you told me...but I'm saying it now. I'm very proud of you, Aris Collier, and you're going to be great."

He waited for a reply, but she remained silent.

His shoulders slumped. "You still mad at me?"

He watched as she continued staring at him, staring through him. "No," she finally said with a small smile.

"Friends?"

As soon as the word left his mouth, he saw the hurt appear in her eyes and it made him feel like shit all over again.

"Are we?" She glanced down at her hands before she looked up with a mixture of hurt and anger in her eyes. "Because if what you said to me is really what you think of me—"

"It's *not*," he said quickly, holding her gaze. "I was

being a dick and I'm sorry. You didn't deserve that."
He paused and grabbed her hand. "And you know
what I really think? I think you are a sweetheart, and
you're a good friend. I mean, look how you've been
there for Kim...and you said you didn't even like her
all that much..."

She laughed, and the sound made him smile again.

"Plus, you're fucking *talented*...I mean, look at you.
All Hollywood now, jetting out to L.A. for school and
doing your thing. And *you* did that. You. All on your
own. So hell yeah, I'm proud of you. Shit, I'm lucky to
know you."

"All right, all right," she said, laughing again. "Now
you're just kissing my ass..."

He leaned back, trying his best not to allow the
sudden image of his mouth on the curve of her sweet
ass to deter him from the goal of his visit—her
forgiveness. "So you forgive me?"

Aris observed him for a long moment before she
slowly nodded. To Luke, it seemed that she really did
forgive him and that she was willing to let it go. That
was good enough for him because he had run out of
words to say to make things right between them.

As he stood up and moved to make himself
comfortable on her sofa, Aris pressed play on her DVR
Grinning, Luke glanced at the now goofy expression
on her face and wondered what the hell had she been
up to before he stopped by. He shook his head. It was
always something with her.

Aris spun her chair around until she was facing him
with her back to the television. When her eyes closed,
he shifted his gaze to the screen. An attractive woman

was standing on a stage with a microphone in her hand. As soon as she started singing, Luke noticed Aris tilt her head in concentration. Shortly after, two of the show's judges pressed a button and their chairs automatically rotated to face the singer. Aris, on the other hand, was still facing Luke, her eyes still closed and her lips tightly pressed together. A few seconds later, the singer belted out a long note and Aris swung her chair around and opened her eyes.

"I knew it!" she yelled, pointing at the screen.

Luke shook his head again. He really didn't want to know, but he had to ask. "Knew what, Moody?"

"She looks exactly the way I pictured her as she was singing. I wasn't going to turn my chair for her at first, but I don't know...she's got something in her voice I like and that last note did it for me..."

Aris paused the judges' commentary while she explained the premise of the show to Luke and caught him up on the blind auditions. He wasn't able to follow most of her rambling, but he didn't dare interrupt her; he was just glad that she was talking to him again.

"Wanna be a judge?" she asked, excitedly.

"Nah, you got it," he replied, yawning as the day's travel finally caught up with him. "I'll just camp out here and watch."

"Ugh, you're no fun."

He grinned and closed his eyes.

To his surprise, Luke felt Aris join him on the sofa. She sat on the other end and grabbed a throw pillow from the adjacent chair. Placing it in her lap, she opened her arms, gesturing for him to lay his head on her lap. Luke shifted his body and pressed his head against the pillow and stretched out as best he could, his legs hanging off the other end of the sofa. Aris pressed play on the remote, reduced the volume and settled into the cushioned corner to finish watching the competition before he closed his eyes again.

When Luke felt Aris's hand casually stroking his head, his stress instantly dissolved. He really wasn't planning to actually fall asleep, but he couldn't help himself. She just had that effect.

That thought plagued him as he drifted to sleep.

An hour later, he was awakened by the harsh buzz of his phone. When he pulled it from the case on his hip, Jessica's face was on the screen.

Luke still felt Aris's hand on his head, but it wasn't moving. Her breathing was quiet and even.

She had fallen asleep too.

The call rolled to voicemail.

Easing up carefully so he wouldn't wake her, Luke debated returning Jessica's call and finally decided it would be best to call her from his apartment. He had been back in town for hours, and Jessica was probably wondering why he hadn't called to let her know he'd arrived safely. It was the first time he'd ever broken their unspoken travel protocol.

The blue message light appeared, but Luke didn't bother to check the voicemail. He stood and stretched just as Aris began stirring. She looked at him curiously.

"You're leaving?"

It was the subtle sadness he heard in her voice that made Luke wonder what they were really doing, what was really going on between them. Though Aris had made no attempt to correct him earlier when he said kissing her had been a mistake, Luke sensed that, if he wanted to do it again—which he definitely did—she wouldn't stop him.

"Yeah, it's almost eight, and I gotta call Jessica," he replied. "Let her know I made it home safely."

Her eyes darted to the wall clock.

"It's already eight?" she asked before she palmed her face with her hands and cursed. Standing abruptly, she nodded and walked him to the foyer, giving him a weak smile when she opened the door. "Later."

The door shut as soon as he crossed the landing.

Damn, what was that about?

Luke let out a long sigh. Those moods of hers were something else. One minute she's asking him if he's leaving, sounding like she wanted him to stay, and the next minute she's bent because it's later than she thought and panicking like...

Luke's jaw tightened at the possibility of why she would suddenly be so concerned with the time, so quick to rush him out of her place and, more specifically...*who* could make her do that.

He raised his hand to knock, wanting answers to questions that were none of his concern, that he had no business asking.

And then his phone buzzed against his hip again.

Lowering his hand, he stepped back from the door and walked home.

~ 15 ~

"Where to?" Devin asked.

Luke slid into the passenger's seat of Devin's truck. "Doesn't matter. As long as it's close. I'm starving."

Devin exited the gym parking lot of the fitness center and cruised to the first restaurant they could find that was still serving breakfast. They had just finished a series of pickup games that lasted a lot longer than either of them intended. Luke's phone had buzzed over two hours ago with a text from Jessica. After learning that she expected him to be at an impromptu lunch meeting she'd scheduled with three other couples he didn't know and didn't care to meet, he sent a brief reply that she would be on her own.

It had been a stressful few days since Luke had been back in town. Though they were cordial to each other and Jessica made sure they had sex every day as her penance for chucking their vacation for a last-minute meeting, he was still on edge and preferred to keep his distance as much as possible until he found a way to shake off his lingering irritation.

"It's been a long ass time since we lost three pick-up games in a row," Devin said after the server took their orders and walked away. He inched over to the corner of the booth near the window and stretched his legs across the bench. "Guess a week in paradise wasn't enough...where's your head, dude?"

He shrugged and took a sip of water.

Realizing Luke wasn't ready to talk, Devin turned his attention to a group of women sitting in the center of the dining room.

Luke followed his gaze and laughed.

"What?" Devin asked, his eyes never leaving the table of women. "Shit, you ain't talking so I might as well find a date for tonight."

"Aris Collier."

"Who?"

"My head." Luke sat back as Devin faced him. "Her name is Aris Collier."

Devin listened quietly as Luke caught him up on his neighbor nonsense but, after five minutes of his vent session, Devin shook his head and literally called a timeout with a hand gesture. "I let you talk because it's clear you need to get this shit off you but, man to man...you're fucking up. You don't throw away a sure thing for a random...you *know* this. And must I also remind you that, unlike average dudes out here, *your* sure thing has always been clear. *Jessica. Fucking. Knox.* It gets no better than that. So whatever you gotta do to get back on track, do it...fast."

Luke toyed with the salt shaker as Devin continued preaching at him, telling him everything that he'd already told himself a dozen times. He felt as stupid as Devin was making him out to be, but he was still unable to shake the hold Aris had on him.

"Are you listening?"

"Yeah," Luke replied, running a hand over his head. "I know. Believe me, I know. But it's like...it's more than physical with this girl. It's...I don't know, man. I just can't figure her out."

"Luke—"

"No, listen," he said, placing his elbows on the table. "That night I told you I stopped by her place and her ex was there? Dude is standing there sizing me up and the crazy part about it is...I'm ready to stomp a hole in this fool's ass just for being there. And when he left, I'm all in *her* face like she owed me some answers. I swear I felt like a fucking idiot, but I couldn't even stop myself..." Luke shook his head and glanced at his friend. Noticing the amused expression on Devin's face, he frowned. "The fuck are you grinning about?"

"Hold up." Devin laughed. "You got all that energy for a chick you ain't even smashed yet?"

As Devin continued laughing, Luke scowled and flagged the server to refill his water glass.

"Well I'll be damned," Devin said, shaking his head as he stared at Luke in amusement and disbelief. "Now you got me curious. I gotta meet this girl."

Despite the past hour of enduring Devin's pointed jokes, thinly-veiled insults and general inquiries about the value of common sense while they ate, Luke found himself standing at Aris's door fifteen minutes after Devin dropped him off at his apartment.

He wasn't caught up. He just felt like seeing her.

Fuck Devin and his fucking, fucked-up opinion.

Luke knocked twice and Aris appeared seconds later, silently opening the door just enough so he could squeeze through. After locking the door, she moved past him and tucked herself into the corner of the sofa, pulling a knitted throw blanket up to her neck.

Moody strikes again.

Grinning, Luke joined her on the sofa and pulled the bottom of the blanket over her bare legs and feet. "What's up?"

"I'm sick."

After reaching over to place a hand against her forehead, Luke sat back and draped an arm across the back of the sofa. "Nope. Try again."

Peeking over the blanket, she narrowed her eyes and frowned at him. "Figuratively."

Giving up the guessing game, Luke turned his attention to the television. "What are you watching? I didn't take you for the *Lifetime* type."

Her frown deepened as she glared at him with disdain. "First off, I'm not. Second, if you expect to remain a welcomed guest in my home, I suggest you get familiar with *Hope Floats*."

Just as he was about to respond, her home phone rang. Sitting up, she reached for the cordless handset laying on the end table and pressed a button to silence the call without even checking the caller ID. "Bill collector," she replied, her eyes back on the television.

A minute later, more ringing filled the air.

This time, she snatched the phone and answered it. "Listen carefully and let me save you the trouble of blowing up my phone for the next few days...I am broke. Which means there's no money for you now, tomorrow or the day after that so...huh? Oh, hi...umm, sorry about that. I thought you were a bill collector. I'm...uh, how are you?"

Looking my way, she knitted her eyebrows as she listened carefully to the caller. After another pause, she bit her lip, stood and crossed the room to step out onto her patio.

Luke watched as she slid the door closed and turned her back to him. Though he was curious, he kept his eyes trained on her television until she walked back inside and bypassed the sofa to sit in a chair. He waited for her to say something, but she remained quiet, her eyes cast to the floor, twisting her hands.

After several minutes of her silence and fidgeting, he muted the television and faced her. "You good?"

"I gotta be." She sighed and ran a hand over her sloppy ponytail. "My Dad is getting married and his girlfri—his fiancé is pressuring me about coming."

"Okay," Luke replied carefully, noting her troubled expression and the overall change in her demeanor.

At the tone of his voice, she lifted her head and held his gaze. "I'm happy for him. It's what he wants, so..." She moved to sit next to him on the sofa, leaning her head back against the cushions as she released another heavy sigh. "At first, the wedding was supposed to be in Savannah, but now it's going to be at some place in Hilton Head and she's rented villas for all the guests and the whole nine. Anyway, it's this weekend and I told her that I'm busy with work and I wouldn't be able to make it, but she keeps insisting that I—" Blinking, she glared at Luke. "What's so funny?"

"Next weekend, I'll be in Savannah. My cousin is taking a job overseas, and my aunt insisted on a bon voyage slash family gathering."

Tilting her head, Aris raised an eyebrow. "You got people in Savannah?"

"A few are there, but most of them are in Atlanta where I'm from."

Slightly turning away, she glanced at him from the corner of her eye. "And you're a Cowboys fan…why?"

"Because I always have been. Always will be."

"Traitor," she said, shaking her head in contempt. "And you claim to be from the A…shame on you."

"Says the girl who proudly rocked a blue-and-white tee with a big ass star on the front of it not too long ago," he replied, laughing.

"Proud? No, sir. I was just being polite as a guest in foreign territory. I bleed black and red…know that. Falcons all day."

"Georgia peach? Nice…" He nodded appreciatively. "Your stock just went up a few points."

"Yeah," she replied, shifting her gaze toward the silent television. "I was born and raised in Savannah. Where my Dad's people are from."

He simply nodded at her last statement, sensing her discomfort. "What do you think you're going to do?"

"Not show up. Piss them off." She looked down at

her hands again and grinned. "It's my thing."

"Not that it's any of my business, but if your lack of a plane ticket is the biggest issue here, I got you."

"Luke, no...you've done enough for me with the car. I can't let you give—"

"Jessica was supposed to fly with me, but she's not going to make it so...no need for a round-trip ticket to go to waste, right?"

She sat quietly, watching him. After a few moments, she grabbed his hand and smiled. "As long as you let me pay the change fee...deal?"

"You don't have to—"

She pinched the skin on the back of his hand and laughed when he pulled away. "Deal?"

"Fine," he said, rubbing his hand. "So you're flying to Savannah with me?"

He watched as her eyes changed again in spite of the smile on her face. "I'm flying to Savannah with you."

Ringing filled the air again. She groaned, and he watched as she absently stared at the phone. On the fifth ring, she finally answered and, just as before, she stood and walked out onto the patio, shutting the door behind her. Assuming it was another call about her father's wedding, Luke stretched out of the sofa and grabbed the remote to find something else to watch.

Ten minutes later, Aris rushed back inside and told him he had to leave as she kept moving down the hall and out of sight.

Shocked, Luke didn't move right away.

"Hey," she yelled to him. "Would you mind locking the bottom handle on your way out? Thanks!"

Damn.

She'd never put him out so abruptly before, so what the hell was this about?

Standing, he strolled down the hall. "Moody?"

"What?" she yelled. "I'm in here!"

He continued in the direction of her voice and peeked into a bedroom. Stepping inside, his eyes were immediately drawn to her bed, which was half-made and king-sized. It dominated the room, covered by a patterned comforter and a ridiculous number of pillows. The room was messy as hell, but it still somehow felt welcoming and comfortable...like her.

Moving toward her walk-in closet, he spotted her quickly going through an unorganized rack of clothing, clearly searching for something specific and annoyed at her inability to find it.

Amused, he leaned against the doorframe. "Are you on your way out or something?"

"Yes," she replied, pulling two dresses off the rack. "I'm sorry...what did you say?"

"Going out?"

"No," she said, squeezing past him to lay the two dresses on her unmade bed. She looked up at him with an embarrassed expression on her face. "Excuse the mess...I didn't have time—"

Grinning, Luke held up both hands. "No judgment."

As she rushed over to a rather ornate floor mirror in the corner of the room with one of the dresses pressed against her body, Luke realized he had never seen her in a dress before...or dressed up at all. After tossing it back on the bed, she yanked a rubber band from her hair and ran her fingers through the tangled mess.

Still leaning against the closet doorframe, he titled his

head and stared, surprised at her sudden concern for her appearance. "Moody, you look fine. What are you getting all dressed up for anyway if you're not going anywhere?"

Moving back to the bed, she held both dresses up by the hanger and faced him. "Black or green?"

Raising an eyebrow, he crossed his arms. "Neither."

"Seriously, Luke...which one is best?"

"Why?"

"Because Marcel is on his way over."

He twisted his mouth, still staring at her.

"Which one?" she asked impatiently as she turned her head side-to-side to look at each one.

"Put them both on, so I can see."

She finally looked at him, her eyes wide. "What?"

"Put them on."

She didn't move right away, observing him to see if he was serious or not. When he didn't say more, she tossed her head back and let out an exasperated sigh before rushing into her bathroom with both dresses.

Removing his phone from its case, Luke checked messages while he waited. He hadn't expected her to change so quickly, so when she opened the door and stepped out he was still busy replying to an urgent email from Devin. After he pressed SEND, he finally focused on Aris.

She'd chosen to put on the black one first, and he didn't bother to disguise his desire...or ignore the stirrings of jealousy in his gut that she was getting all dolled up for Marcel. She looked as amazing in the dress as he expected she would, and he knew it was childish but he wanted to see her in it first.

"So?" she asked, twirling around.

"So," he replied, his eyes everywhere the dress didn't cover. "Wear the green."

"Seriously?" She glanced down at her body to inspect the dress before she looked up. "What's wrong with this one?"

Closing the distance between them, his eyes revealed everything that was right with it and she took a step back in understanding.

"Fine," she said in a low voice. "Thanks."

He took another step forward, his gaze dropping to her lips. She took another step back.

"Luke, we can't. Like we said, this is a mistake."

Twisting his mouth, he backed away from her. They walked quietly out of her bedroom, and she followed him as he continued to the front door. Stepping out into the cool air, he turned to face her and she caught his gaze right before he let his eyes travel every inch of her body.

"Goodnight, Luke."

He nodded in response, battling with the idea that they were only friends and nothing more. Dragging his lustful eyes back up to her anxious face, he did his best let his feelings go and reinstate their platonic status... but he honestly wasn't sure how much longer his resolve would last.

"Enjoy your night," he finally said as he walked away. "Wear the green."

~ 16 ~

Aris wore the black dress.

When Marcel arrived and saw the full effect of it along with her hair, makeup and stilettos, he informed her that she looked too good to be in the house tonight.

Which was what she was hoping he'd say.

The last thing Aris wanted to do was remain in her apartment after what had almost happened between her and Luke…again. What she needed was to be as far away from Cypress Lake as possible so she could focus on enjoying the attention and affection of the great guy she had who *wasn't* involved with anyone else but her.

Fortunately, her escape plan worked.

Marcel whisked her away and couldn't keep his eyes and hands off of her the entire evening.

Too bad she couldn't keep her mind off Luke and the fact that she would be flying home with him…

Not to mention that her father's wedding in a few

days, and Aris still wasn't sure how she really felt about it.

She had never met Celeste in person. The woman had dug up Aris's abandoned social media account and sent her an inbox message out of the blue one day. Aris noticed it weeks later and, after putting it off for another few weeks, she finally replied to the stranger's message. A surprise phone call came soon after.

Celeste had been persistent, eager to know the only child of the man who had captured her heart.

During the entire phone exchange, Aris was pleasant but indifferent. In her mind, there was no need to connect. There had been so many women before this one that Aris no longer had the patience to endure another. None of them had managed to get her father to the altar...what made this one so certain of her happy ending?

When Celeste asked her to hold on and her father's voice came on the line a moment later, Aris quickly realized that this one *was* different. It was the first time in her recent memory that her father actually sounded happy. He was even talking to her as opposed to his habit of talking *at* her since she was a small child. During that bizarre conversation, there were no terse updates or unwinnable debates between them...just a free flow of information and genuine interest from him about what she was currently doing with her life... all without judgment.

Because he'd finally gotten a life of his own.

For as long as Aris could remember, she'd been a disappointment to him. She was the sole source of the permanent crease between his brow and the natural downturn of his mouth because she'd never been good enough...she'd never been her mother. Actually, no one on Earth had ever been Lydia Collier or lived up to the ghost her father kept alive every day, the woman who had the ability to consistently make Tony Collier smile, laugh and joke.

Except Celeste.

With Celeste, he was happy.

Something Aris never thought possible.

Celeste was also slightly obnoxious. No matter how much distance Aris tried to create, Celeste worked tirelessly to close the gap, making it her personal mission to be the bridge between father and daughter. As a barren woman, Celeste viewed Aris as her only chance at solidifying the family she'd always hoped for but sadly couldn't physically achieve. It was an understandable desire for her to want to put the three of them in a bowl, add water and stir, but Aris wanted no parts of it and never hesitated to excuse herself from every invitation for holidays and gatherings.

She was working.

She was sick.

She couldn't afford to fly home.

The last excuse was an easy one for them to resolve, but they never did. Aris never questioned why — if they wanted her home so badly — they didn't simply send her a round trip plane ticket. She already knew why.

Her father hadn't changed *that* much.

The more he aged, the more critical and resentful he became. Tony Collier had never wanted kids. He'd only agreed to one because he could never deny her mother anything. When she died, he had no idea what to do with a precocious four-year-old but he did the best he could. He was a great provider and she never wanted for anything...except to *feel* wanted. Instead, she always felt like the glorious burden he carried, the perpetual slammed door to every opportunity that had ever come his way. Most of all, she felt like a poor substitute and the permanent link to his pain.

Despite those feelings, she never doubted that he loved her. Of course, he did. He was her father, and she was his only kid. But Aris was pretty clear every time he laid eyes on her that he secretly wished she had never been born.

And by the time she made it to middle school, Aris had sort of wished that too.

"We're almost there," Marcel said, pulling her from the past. "Are you all right?"

"Yeah," she replied with a small smile. "I'm great."

As they fell back into an uncomfortable silence, she kept her eyes on the road. When she suddenly heard him ask if she'd rather cancel their after-dinner plans and go home, she placed a hand on his arm and insisted that she still wanted to take a stroll through Klyde Warren Park and hang out a little longer.

It was the most honest thing she'd said all night...

Never mind the discomfort of her not-designed-for-walking stilettos and her complete inability to deal with the real reason why she didn't want him to take her home.

When they finally arrived at the park, Aris took in the splendor and her lips parted in a genuine smile. From the Pavilion and Great Lawn to the Botanical Gardens, Reading & Games Courtyard and the

Children's Park, Klyde Warren Park was indeed a spectacular addition to the district. As a woman who always celebrated art and beauty in all its forms, she wholeheartedly agreed with Marcel that it was a magnificently innovative way to bring green space into the heart of downtown Dallas.

As they approached a bench, she finally locked eyes with Marcel, who was in the midst of yet another one of his endless stares. Touching the back of her neck, she smiled at him awkwardly. "What?"

"You look stunning tonight." Backing up his words, Marcel's eyes raked over her body in appreciation. "If it isn't obvious."

Genuinely flattered, she smiled. "Thank you."

"I'm sure you're ready to sit for a while. It was pretty insensitive of me to suggest coming here without making sure you had another pair of comfortable shoes to walk in. I assumed maybe you did."

"Where?" she asked, showing him her small clutch. "Can't see how I could possibly fit shoes in here."

He grinned. "Don't they sell those flats that you can put in a zip lock bag or something?" When she laughed, he shrugged indifferently. "I don't know what you call them. I was out one night at a club and saw some woman break them out of her bag. One minute, she was limping and, the next minute, she was line dancing like nobody's business."

"Line dancing?" she asked, raising an eyebrow. "What kind of geriatric club was that...and, the better question is, why were *you* there?"

He laughed. "Yeah, I know. Don't ask."

"I'll give you a pass. These days, there's no escaping

all the shuffles, slides and wobbles going around…"

She paused to look at him, narrowing her eyes. "*Please* tell me you don't wobble."

"Never have and never will," he replied as they laughed together.

Settling next to him on the bench, she finally felt at ease for the first time all night. "Thank you. This was a great idea. I'm having a wonderful time *and* I'm totally proud that I managed to conquer these heels without once busting on my ass." Throwing her hands in the air, she began to wiggle in place. "Winning!"

"I'm glad to hear that," he replied, watching her. "I was kind of worried that I'd lost you about two hours ago. You seemed, I don't know…distracted. Until now. I hadn't planned on saying anything. Just wanted to give you time to work through it on your own."

Meeting his gaze, she reached over and squeezed his hand. "I appreciate that. I'm okay."

"I'm glad," he replied as his eyes swept her face. "And I'm also happy that you're here with me."

Sensing that he might kiss her, Aris pulled back and turned her attention to the small group of people sitting on several blankets in the grass. "I can't believe how safe it feels out here. It's not often that you can hang out in a public park at night without worrying about getting robbed."

"Yes, they've done a great job with this place," he said as he suddenly stood from the bench. "It's a lot more active during the day, with food trucks and activities and all. Maybe the next time our schedules permit, we can come back and check it out."

"Sure," she said, smiling up at him as he helped her

stand. "I'd like that."

Once they returned to his car, they listened to a new jazz station as Marcel drove up the highway to Frisco. When he pulled up to her driveway, her plan was to hop out so he could keep rolling but Marcel was a gentleman. After parking, he walked her to her front door and made sure she was safely inside.

"I had a great time tonight, Marcel."

"My pleasure, sweetheart."

Suddenly feeling awful about her distant behavior most of the night, she stepped closer and, without pause, placed a gentle kiss against his lips. One that let him know that she liked and appreciated him, but one that also hopefully made it clear that the jury was still out on getting physical. Stepping back, she observed his expression to see if he'd gotten the message. Noticing the slightly disappointed look in his eyes, he apparently had. "Thanks again. Get home safely."

After closing and locking the door, Aris lightly banged her head against it a few times before she walking into her kitchen on a mission to empty the pint of Jack underneath her cabinet.

All she wanted to do was forget that she'd ruined a completely wonderful night. Every time Marcel tried to touch her or kiss her, all she could think about was Luke and the last time he'd done what her date had wanted to do all evening.

Placing the liquor bottle on the counter, she poured the dark liquid into a tiny glass. Closing her eyes, she tried to quell the waves that had been disturbing her since Luke left her apartment by lifting the shot to her lips and downing it quickly. As it burned a path down her throat, she silently chastised herself, knowing that her current surge had everything to do with what happened earlier with Luke and nothing at all to do with the last few hours she'd spent with Marcel.

An image of him appeared in her mind, specifically the look of disappointment that Marcel had done his best to hide all night.

"Of course, he was disappointed," she mumbled to herself. "You dress it all up and then refuse to let him play with it? Who does that? Ugh...you're the *worst*..."

She poured herself another shot, filling it to the rim so that it spilled over a little as she brought it to her lips and tossed her head back. Shaking her head, she licked her lips, ready to go for another round but a series of hard knocks on her front door made her jump.

As the knocks kept coming, she tried to focus, the alcohol already affecting her senses. As she moved to the door, a sudden, nagging feeling made her pause.

Who else could it be but Marcel?

He was probably back to convince her to let him inside....literally and figuratively.

She could certainly do that but then what would she say to him afterwards? She didn't want to lie, but she definitely wasn't in the mood for truth tonight either.

Rubbing her forehead, she stood motionless in the kitchen as the knocking continued. She figured Marcel would eventually give up and leave, but he just started knocking louder and more aggressively instead, like it wasn't almost ten p.m. and she didn't have neighbors.

Grabbing the pint of Jack, she took a quick swig which only served to fuel her rising irritation that he couldn't take the hint that the night was over. By the time she yanked the door open, she was ready to deliver the brutal truth but she choked on her words as soon as Luke came into view.

The minute Luke saw her, he caught his breath. Then he took in the full show on display that he wasn't privileged to have seen earlier—the perfect makeup, the towering stilettos, the gorgeous hair—and he was suddenly enraged.

Because none of it had been for him.

And she chose to wear that fucking black dress.

Stepping into her apartment without permission, he closed the door and turned the lock before moving close enough to feel the heat from her body. Before she could step out of his reach, he hooked an arm around her waist and brought her lips to his. His hand slipped from her waist to her ass as she kissed him back, her arms looping around his neck as they teased and toyed with each other. Nipping at her lips, he felt her arms loosen before her hands dropped to his chest as she impatiently pushed him back against the nearest wall. Aligning her body to his, she rose to her toes and attacked his neck with her mouth as her hands fumbled with the buttons of his shirt. Her sudden aggression turned him on even more, and he would have smiled but she slipped her tongue into his mouth and made him groan instead.

Palming her ass with one hand while lifting the other hand to her breast, he teased her protruding nipple with the pad of his thumb. She was still kissing him, making him dizzy, but her aggression waned as she slowly melted against him, her moans and her sighs driving him crazy.

Pulling back, she looked at him with hooded eyes. In response, he attempted to guide her to the nearest piece of furniture but she stopped him, tilting her head toward her bedroom before she captured his lips again.

They stumbled down the hall, not once coming up for air until they were inside her bedroom, the corner of her bed stopping them. Reaching for the bottom of his shirt, he felt her hands push his out of the way as she bit her lip and stared up at him. Dropping his arms to his sides, he watched as she quickly unbuttoned and removed his shirt and the minute he felt her soft hands run over his bare arms, he reached for her but she forced his hands back to his sides and continued to torture him.

Lifting the white cotton of his undershirt, she dipped her head and kissed and licked her way up his stomach and chest until he was finally naked from the waist up. He tried reaching for her again, but she swatted his hands away and smiled, lightly tracing the contours of his upper body with her fingers. When the tip of her nail grazed his nipple, he cursed and ended her game, removing everything from her body with the exception of her jewelry and heels before placing her in the center of her bed. He kissed every exposed area until his mouth finally clamped over her nipple and he slipped his hand between her legs to caress her clit.

"Fuck..." Slipping a finger inside, he stroked her slowly until she began moving back and forth against his hand. He shifted his mouth from her nipple to her lips and kissed her until her grinding was in rhythm with the strokes of their tongues. Lifting his head, he watched as she moaned when his finger found her clit again, circling it over and over until she tensed and sighed his name.

Releasing a tortured breath, he slowly pulled away and shook his head, reluctant to pause but knowing it had to be done. "Do you have protection?"

She nodded quickly, pointing toward her nightstand. He sat up and pulled a condom from her drawer before he opened the package and quickly covered himself. Back in bed, he kissed her slowly as she spread her legs and welcomed him into her folds. His intent had been to take his time with her, but she made it immediately evident that his carefulness wasn't what she wanted. Whispering everything she wanted him to do to her in his ear, she broke him down until he tossed the pretense aside and did exactly as she instructed. Just as ravenous, she met him stroke for stroke until her body shook, drowning him as he held on and rode the waves with her.

Still buried, he carefully rolled to his back, pulling her with him so he could hold her as she recovered. Instead, she sat up and rode the hell out of him until he forced her to her back again and drilled her into the bed. When she tightened around him and exploded for the second time, her tremors and moans finally drove him to his own release, the intensity of his orgasm forcing her name from his lips over and over in a voice he barely recognized as his own.

Breathing hard, he slipped out of her and collapsed

onto the bed. A moment later, he forced himself to get up and toss the condom. Easing back onto the bed, his heart was still pounding as he peeked over at her. Eyes closed, she was still breathing heavily with a look of satisfaction on her face. Settling onto his back, he pulled her to him and they lay quietly with her head against his chest. As he played with her hair, he was slightly hesitant to say anything, suddenly regretting how aggressive he had been, but then he thought back to how she had matched his intensity with equal fervor and a small smile touched his lips. He couldn't believe she wore him out…and he *still* wasn't satisfied.

A part of him had expected that being inside of Aris once would be enough to get over his infatuation, to finally lose that edge he'd been feeling for weeks since they'd met. In his mind, it was something he'd given too much thought to, something he simply needed to resolve so he could move on, get her out of his system and continue the life he was living with Jessica before Aris invited him into hers. Tonight, his only goal had been to douse the flames but, looking at her now, all he'd done was expose the answer to a question he'd had no business posing.

And now that he knew, he couldn't *un*-know it.

What the fuck was he supposed to do now?

Aris stirred against him and snuggled closer. Even in that moment, he couldn't stop himself from needing her again. He wanted to touch her, to replace what had just happened between them with something less dicey and perverse, something that would be a truer reflection of what he wasn't quite ready to put into words but he still wanted her to know.

He opened his mouth to speak, but everything he thought to say seemed inadequate, selfish. So he said nothing. Minutes later, she pulled away to look at him. He held her gaze, pleased when a hint of a smile suddenly appeared on her beautiful face. After placing a soft kiss on his cheek, she rested her head against his chest and snuggled even closer until she fit perfectly against him. His pulse began to race, a pressure in his chest building so strong that he suddenly felt like he was suffocating...until she lifted a hand and placed it on his chest over his heart. Though his mind continued to race about everything that had just happened, her touch immediately calmed him...as it always did.

He found his voice. "Why did you let me?"

"Not sure exactly." She fell silent until a giggle escaped her lips. "Seemed like you kinda needed it."

"Always with the jokes." Pulling away from her, Luke's hand tilted her head so he could see her eyes and she would know that he was serious. "What about you? What do you need?"

She shifted her gaze before ducking her head and snuggling back against him. "Nothing."

He did his best to relax and not press her for answers, but then his pulse sped up again and it took everything in him not to slip inside her again and cheapen the moment. He'd already fucked up once; he had no intention of doing that again. For all he knew, this could be the last time he saw her. Her "nothing" response disturbed him, like something had shifted for her and maybe not in a good way. Even if he was in this alone, there was no way in hell they could go back to being just friends. Shit, he wouldn't allow it.

Caught off guard by the intensity of his desperation, he pulled her even closer against him. Just the thought of not seeing her again, not being with her like this again, inside her again...

Fuck that.

He couldn't let her go.

"Sorry I was so rough...did I hurt you?"

Before he could stop it, a laugh bubbled up and tumbled from his lips at her question. His mind immediately flashed through every moment of passion they'd experienced and he grinned. As he dropped a hand to brush his palm over the curve of her ass, he was more than happy to know that the intensity between them was mutual. "In the best way."

He could feel her smile though her head still rested against his chest. Suddenly, she shifted and caught his eyes. "Can I hurt you again?"

Though he was more than willing, Luke hesitated as the reality of their situation reared its head. This was wrong and he wasn't proud of himself, of the entire situation but, as her lips touched his and she spread her legs for him again, he realized that telling her no was something he was pretty sure he would never be able to do. Shutting his eyes, he slipped inside of her and blocked out the guilt as the pleasure took over. Soon, nothing else mattered as he traveled deeper and deeper within her walls. With her wrapped tightly around him, it was like he had finally discovered something he never knew he could feel...and he was certain that he'd never be able to get enough.

Slowing his stroke to an agonizing pace, he took his time to explore her body and to do everything he'd ever thought about doing to her since the night she'd fed him the worst breakfast he'd ever tasted. It wasn't long before he lost control again and they were consumed with each other, the energy between them just as erotic but somehow much more passionate. As he plunged into her, again and again, he was stunned because, in that moment, he knew that what was happening was more than an ego trip or a way for him to escape his issues. It was way more than just sex.

As Luke lost himself in Aris, he was released from every doubt, every disappointment, every obligation, every worry, every fear...

In that moment, Luke let it all go.

With Aris, he found peace.

~ 17 ~

"Did I *not* tell you to leave her ass alone?"

Luke continued toying with the straw in his glass, understanding Devin's frustration but not moved by it. He'd already beaten himself up enough since it had happened. After leaving Aris's bed and climbing into his own, the weight of what he had done came crashing down and robbed him of sleep for the past three nights. Deciding to come clean to Devin had been his attempt to lift some of the pressure of having to deal with the fallout on his own.

"Dude…are you even listening?"

Luke pulled his gaze from the water glass and looked Devin in the eyes and nodded though he hadn't heard a word of what he'd just said. "I hear you."

Devin sat back, his expression one of disbelief. Luke understood why. In all the years Devin had known him, cheating on Jessica was the very last thing he or anyone else would have thought he could do.

"I don't know what's up with you lately, but you need to fix that shit like asap." Devin leaned forward, placing his elbows on the table in the manner he usually did when he was consulting a wayward client and initiating damage control. "If that means fucking her a few more times, so be it. Whatever it takes to get over it. Even the best pussy gets tired after a while..."

Luke nodded despite already knowing otherwise.

"Damn it, man...I knew I should've forced you to work this shit out back in college. You ain't had new pussy in like a decade so it was bound to happen." Shaking his head, he frowned in confusion. "But what I don't get is...why now?"

He shrugged.

Because he honestly wasn't sure why.

For the past few days, he'd been asking himself the very same question. He'd always been faithful in and out Jessica's presence. Honestly, he'd just never been that pressed about other women. All it took was a quick assessment of the contender and, without fail, Jessica won each and every time.

No one had ever been worth it before.

No one until Aris.

The crazy part is that if he had met Aris at any other point before now, he wouldn't have even looked twice at her. So the only thing left that made sense was that he was on some rebellious, tantrum-type shit. He didn't really believe himself to be that shallow, that childish...but he also couldn't deny the increasing discomfort he felt in his relationship with Jessica and everything being with her represented.

"I don't know," he finally replied as Devin shook his head at him again. "Seriously, all I know is that I'm headed to Savannah tomorrow and Aris is tagging along because Jessica canceled on me for some chick trip with her girls in New York."

Devin nodded and leaned back in his chair. "Sounds like a perfect opportunity to resolve this shit. Get it out of your system and get back to your life...a *great* life. Try to remember that when you're balls deep this weekend...that this is temporary. Keep it simple and discreet...got it?"

Luke nodded, still unsure of everything. "Got it."

"You're what?"

Aris shifted her eyes away from the perplexed expression on Marcel's handsome face and focused her attention on the artifact hanging on the painted wall just behind his head.

"I'm moving to Los Angeles in December," she said again, grateful when the server appeared with the check. She attempted to grab it, but Marcel's hand shot out and pulled it in his direction. Her eyes softened as she looked at him. "Please. Let me get it this time."

"You will do no such thing." He removed his wallet, all traces of his surprise at her admission now gone.

As he counted out bills, Aris filled the silence by explaining more than he probably cared to know — about her interests, about applying for school, about getting accepted. He listened quietly but attentively, still without expression. When she finished, she waited anxiously for his response though she realized that he didn't owe her one.

He didn't owe her anything at this point.

"Well, I guess congratulations are in order." He finally smiled. "The way you speak about your work, this definitely appears to be a dream come true for you. I wish you all the best."

Aris blinked. Twice.

Marcel was a better man than she'd realized.

Confirmation that ending things with him before they even began was indeed the right decision.

"Marcel, I'm sorry—"

"There's no need to apologize, Aris. We were just dating. I'll admit that I was hoping for something more permanent with you, but life happens and this definitely sounds like an opportunity you can't pass up. I'm disappointed, but I can accept that." He stood and helped her from the booth. "You're an amazing woman, Aris Collier, and it was a pleasure to have crossed paths with you."

She stepped into his arms for a hug, feeling the same way about him. "Likewise, Marcel Baylor."

Leaving the restaurant, they parted ways amicably. No kiss. No longing stares. No promises to keep in touch. It was a clean break. And she was proud of herself because this was the first situation where she didn't allow things to linger, unfinished. It was what she wanted her life to be about from now on—the unwavering discipline and natural ability to always move forward. Though she accomplished that tonight with Marcel, the real challenge was still ahead...

Could she truly move on from Luke...especially now that she was in love with him?

Aris wasn't quite sure when love happened but it had and pretending otherwise was useless. Ending up in bed with him had been a given. They'd been dancing around it for weeks, so it was bound to happen. And though it was wrong and she still did not regret one moment of what they shared, she also knew that it could never happen again. She had enough to deal with and really didn't care to own that particular badge of shame—homewrecker.

She had been many things in her life but never any man's side piece. Aris fully expected this to end badly not only because of karma's inevitability but also because of the truth—what could she possibly offer a man like Luke? Yes, the sex was great between them but it was one time...well, technically, *three* times in one night...but her lulls were sure to return and then he would discover that she was even moodier than he realized. So why bother?

Bottom line, Luke belonged with Jessica and there was no way Aris could or should compete with that. She would never be right for him...it was true the night they met and truer now that she'd come to know him. Not to mention that Aris really was everything that Luke said she was. What she'd just done to Marcel was just one of many prime examples. How long would it be before she met another guy under the guise of "friendship?"

David, Shane, Ralph, Luke, Marcel—she couldn't help herself. It was in her nature.

She had to leave them all behind. Especially Luke.

Her gut twisted at the thought of losing him, but she quickly chastised herself...because he wasn't hers.

So the only thing left for her to do was stay focused and try not to catch any more feelings for him than she already had. It was just one weekend...she would simply fly to Savannah, handle the wedding, fly back, pack up everything she owned, leave Dallas behind and never look back...

It was for the best.

Always forward.

~ *18* ~

Aris peeked through the blinds for the fourth time.

Stepping away from the window, she forced herself to park her ass on the sofa and chill...something she hadn't been able to do since she made it home from her final date with Marcel.

Driving home, she had felt a *nothingness*. It was so profound that she took to her bed as soon as she locked herself inside her apartment. No shower. No television. No mannequins. Just darkness, silence and more of the nothingness she felt inside.

The next morning, she called in sick to the boutique and texted Kim that she needed a day off. Kim responded right away, recommending three, and Aris had been home in bed since...thinking.

She'd been doing way too much of that lately.

Running a hand over her hair, Aris jumped when she suddenly heard a hard knock at her front door. After taking a deep breath, she walked over and opened it to see Luke smiling back at her.

"Hey."

"Hey," she replied, letting him in.

He looked around the room. "Where's your stuff?"

"In my room. I'll get it...I don't have much."

After a few minutes, Aris appeared with a large, rolling suitcase and two duffle bags.

He grinned. "Not much, huh?"

After assessing her baggage, she looked up at him with a worried expression. "I should probably leave some of this here. I just didn't know what to bring—"

"It's fine, Moody," he said, pulling one of the bags from her shoulder. "Better to be safe than sorry."

She looked at him and finally nodded, watching as he reached for the handle of her suitcase. Following him to the doorway, she bumped into him when he stopped abruptly to look at her.

"You're in a place."

She twisted her mouth. "No, I'm not."

"Yes, you are," he replied. "Do me a favor?"

Looking away, she nodded for him to continue.

"Relax." He waited until she stopped fidgeting and finally locked eyes with him before he spoke again. "I know things are complicated between us now after our night together, but this trip is still about me helping you to get to Hilton Head for your Dad's wedding. I'm still your friend, Moody. And believe it or not, that's more important to me than anything else going on with us right now...okay?"

She took a deep breath. "Okay."

"Stop worrying and just enjoy yourself." He gently

pressed a finger against the wrinkle between her eyebrows until the skin smoothed. "When's the last time you had a break, anyway?"

She thought about telling him about the last forty-eight hours she'd spent buried in her bed but decided to keep it to herself and not respond.

"Exactly. Take advantage. Sleep late, eat everything in sight, hang out, get wasted, whatever. That's what I'm planning to do."

Feeling more at ease, she smiled at him. "What happens in Savannah, stays in Savannah?"

"That's my Moody," he said, winking. "I knew there was something I liked about you."

"Shotgun!"

Luke shook his head.

"What?" she asked, innocently. "It's still a thing."

"Yeah. If you're eight."

Sticking out her tongue, Aris ducked her head and dropped into the passenger side of Luke's rental car. After pre-programming her favorite FM stations into every available button, she sat back and gazed out of the window. It was a beautiful, unseasonably warm day in Savannah, and she was thrilled for the reprieve from the chill she'd escaped in Dallas.

"Where to?" Luke asked without looking at her as he merged onto the interstate.

"Yeah, about that…"

He chuckled. "I got it."

She turned her body to face him and observed the satisfied look on his face. "I'll pay you back."

"No need," he replied, indifferently. "I took a wild guess that maybe you would need an out...you know, in case things got rough with your family and you'd rather not stay in the villas with them."

"Well, aren't you presumptuous?"

He grinned. "But was I right?"

"Hmm..."

Laughing, he set the cruise control and leaned his head back against the seat. "So for real...do I need to drop you off there or are you coming with me?"

"Since you *insist*," she replied, smiling. "I'm coming with you."

Reaching into her bag, she pulled out her phone to text Celeste that she was in town but would not be staying in the villas rented for family and friends. After sending the message, she felt such a sense of calm that she audibly sighed.

As always, she had Luke to thank for her relief.

Grabbing his hand, Aris settled against the car seat and kept her gaze on the passing scenery until her eyes grew heavy and she drifted off to sleep the rest of the ride to Luke's hotel...in Hilton Head.

When they arrived at the resort, she tried not to react. Of course, Luke and Jessica would reserve a hotel miles out to enjoy the ocean while they were in town. She had no doubt the two always traveled in style...which was a fortunate thing for her at the moment. Still, Aris couldn't help but think that, in all the years she'd lived in Savannah, she never once experienced the luxury of an ocean-front resort on the coast.

"Hey, what's with the face?" Luke asked, pulling her from her thoughts. "Is this cool or would you prefer a hotel closer to where your family's staying?"

She gave him the side-eye. "Prefer a different hotel? Are you insane? This is great. Besides, I'm with you this weekend. I go where you go."

She noticed that same satisfied expression he had in the car resurface before he smiled at her. Dismissing the warmth of his gaze and her body's instant reaction, she followed him into the lobby and waited as he checked in with the front desk agent. Minutes later, Luke approached with his hand extended to give her a key to the room.

"You're on the fifteenth floor, and I'm right above you on sixteen...Room 1632." He tilted his head and dropped his hand when she didn't accept the room key. "What's wrong?"

"I'm not staying with you?"

The words tumbled out before she could stop them. When he stared at her with no response, she looked away and tucked a strand of hair behind her ear. "I just thought you meant that you had space in your room for me, but it's no big deal...well, actually it kinda *is* a big deal because I can't exactly afford this place and I already owe you so much so it's probably best I find a cheaper place to crash since—"

"There's space for you."

She looked up and caught the smile in his eyes.

"Give me a second," he replied, passing her the key to his room. "I need to cancel this extra room."

Once they arrived in his suite, Aris stared wide-eyed at the sheer size of it. He hadn't been kidding...there was not only space for her but also for ten others.

After parking her rolling suitcase in the corner, she rushed over to the doors to the balcony to take in the view. As she looked out into the Atlantic Ocean, she felt Luke ease into the space behind her. For a brief moment, she closed her eyes, willing herself to hold to the promise she'd made to not catch any more feelings.

Too bad her body refused to cooperate.

"What do you think?"

She did her best not to incline her head, not to ease closer to him so that his mouth would graze her ear, her face, her neck...

His phone buzzed.

When he stepped back, Aris released a sharp breath she hadn't realized she'd been holding. Pressing her lips together, she kept her eyes focused on the crashing waves several stories below while trying not to listen to his conversation.

"Yeah, I got here about an hour ago," Luke said to the caller. "I thought y'all weren't starting until later? Okay, cool. I got a couple of things to handle first and then I'm on my way. Yeah...got it. Peace."

Turning from the window to finally face him, she watched as he began rapidly tapping the screen of his phone. "My brother, Nate," he generously offered as a reply to a question she didn't want to ask. "Looks like the party is starting sooner than I expected."

Disappointed that he would be leaving so soon, she offered him a tentative smile when he finally pulled his eyes away from his phone to look at her. "Sure, no problem. Have a good time. I'll just explore the hotel or watch TV or grab some food—"

"You're welcome to come with me. If you'd like."

Her eyes widened at his suggestion. "Oh, I couldn't just show up like that." She shrugged. "I'll just stay here. I'm fine."

"Okay, but I'd love to have you there with me," he replied, his eyes never leaving her face. "Your choice."

And with that he walked away and made another phone call. She lingered in the living room for another few minutes before opening one of her duffle bags and pulling out a pair of jeans and a slouchy sweater. She had no idea if this party was dressy or casual affair. Holding the jeans in her left hand and the sweater in the other, she walked over to Luke and waited patiently for him to see her choices as he continued chatting on the phone.

When he finally looked up, he approved both with a thumbs up and smiled as he watched her carry her clothes and drag her suitcase into the bathroom to get ready to meet the family.

~ *19* ~

Ten minutes after arriving at the house party, Aris had only one thought—the Donovans were an insanely attractive family...along with the Jacksons, the Stones, the Whitmores, and the Reeds.

It was so many of them, she'd lost count.

Luke was gracious, introducing her as his friend from Dallas. She appreciated that and was even more grateful to not receive vicious stares because Jessica should be there instead of her. On the contrary, nobody mentioned Jessica at all which was odd to say the least.

The first person Aris met was Luke's brother, Nate. He was slightly taller than Luke and as casual and boisterous as Luke was reserved and buttoned-up. Despite the differences, it was apparent that they were as close as siblings could be.

After that, she met a few of Luke's cousins—Daniel, Brian, Dean and Lexi—who welcomed her and made sure she had a drink in her hand at all times. Then there were the elders—Luke's parents, aunts and uncles—and dozens of kids of all ages.

It was beyond overwhelming. As Luke reunited with his family, all Aris wanted to do was find a corner to occupy. However, every time she was even close to succeeding, his younger female cousins invaded her space without permission. Before long, they were pulling her around the backyard, teaching her the latest dances and laughing as she struggled to learn them all. Every so often, wherever he was, whoever he was with, Luke still found her. As soon as he caught her eyes, she would simply smile to let him know that she was okay...because, surprisingly, she really was.

Luke chuckled to himself as he watched Aris, completely surrounded by his crazy-ass cousins. He knew they were a handful, but she seemed to be holding her own and having a good time. He was glad that she decided to tag along. It satisfied him in a way that he couldn't begin to describe.

Strolling over to them, Luke's smile slowly relaxed into a hardened expression when Kirk Jensen slithered his way into the group and eased into Aris's space. Luke didn't interrupt, choosing to watch the familiar scene play out as it had many times in the past.

When they were young, Kirk lived on the same street and attended grade school with Luke's cousins. Luke remembered him as a flashy kid whose parents always showered him with more money than attention. Kirk was also a jerk who loved to take things that weren't his and put his hands where they didn't belong... which was exactly what he was attempting now with Aris until Luke stepped between them and hung his arm around her shoulder.

"Hey," Aris said, smiling up at him.

Luke didn't reply, too busy leveling an icy glare on Kirk. "Long time, man...what's good?"

"Yeah. Really long time. I'm cool, man...in town for a bit, you know...relaxing, taking a break. Actually, I messed around and picked up a new A8 earlier today. I haven't really had time to test her out on the road... still trying to decide if I'll keep it or get something else." Kirk looked at Aris and smiled. "I was just about to ask Aris if she wanted to take a ride with me. Aunt Laura needed some more ice from the store."

"Actually," Luke replied with a smirk. "Aunt Laura just pulled out her famous banana pudding. Matter of fact, I think she baked a few sweet potato pies too."

"Hold up," Aris replied, her eyes widening as she looked up at him. "Did you say sweet potato pie?"

He winked at her. "I did."

"That's all I needed to hear!" she said before taking off toward the house.

Still smirking, Luke shook his head. "She loves dessert. Didn't want her to miss out...you know Aunt Laura's pies never last too long."

"Yeah," Kirk said dryly. "I do."

"Hey, do you mind grabbing some more soda while you're out?" Pulling out his wallet, Luke counted a few bills and extended them to Kirk. "I think that should cover it."

"No problem," Kirk replied, declining the cash. He glanced in the direction Aris went before leveling his gaze on Luke. "Oh yeah, I meant to tell you congrats...I heard you're still living it up in Dallas and heading up a division at Knox Corp. By the way, how's Jessica doing?"

"Thanks. She's good."

"Glad to hear that," Kirk replied flippantly. "Well, tell her I said hello. See you around."

Without bothering to reply, Luke watched as Kirk strolled away and stopped to chat with another friend of the family before Lexi blocked his line of sight.

He lifted his head in acknowledgment. "Hey, Lex."

"Don't 'hey' me...what was that about?"

"What was what about?" he asked, raising a brow.

"You're posturing," Lexi said, grinning wickedly. "So you and Miss Aris are besties or whatever...I get it. What I can't understand is why you feel a need for everyone within a fifty-yard radius to know it."

Luke laughed. "Still the busybody, huh Lex?"

"No. Just very observant." She crossed her arms and stared at him. "Just friends, huh?"

"Yep."

"Bullshit," she replied, chuckling. "Dude, it's all over you. Get your shit together before it interrupts the inheritance you've got waiting on you back in Dallas."

Patting him playfully on the back, Lexi strolled away with a satisfied smile just as Brian yelled for him to bring some rationality to the current college football debate going on between Nate, Dean and Daniel. Dismissing Lexi's unsolicited commentary, Luke joined the guys' colorful exchange that kept him tied up for the next half hour.

Finally excusing himself, he searched for Aris and found her sitting alone in furthest corner of the backyard. Once he made it to her side, he sat without speaking, sensing that quiet was what she needed. He caught himself smiling as they sat in silence. There was something truly special about the way he was beginning to innately "get" her, the way he was able to understand her wants and needs without words ever being spoken.

After a few moments, she reached out and slipped her hand in his. She hadn't even turned her head; she just blindly zeroed in on him like a homing device as if she knew it would be there for her to hold. He smiled.

"I just needed a minute. I got overstimulated."

"It's cool. I get that same feeling every time we all get together." He looked at the crowd of people and grinned. "No explanation needed. Trust me."

"Whatever...you love it." She glanced at him. "It may have been a headache at times, but I bet it was still fun for you though...growing up like this."

"It was. Our grandparents made sure we all stayed close. Family was and is always first."

"The way it should be."

Luke leaned over, nudging her with his shoulder. "You're in a place. Talk to me."

"Just wondering what it would have been like if I had more of that."

"More of what?"

"Family."

A breeze drifted through and tussled her hair about

her head. When the strands settled over her eyes and against her cheek, she lifted her hand and tucked them behind her ears but they escaped again.

"It was basically just me and my Dad," she said, picking up from her last comment. "And his sister was around a lot too. She moved down here to help raise me after her son joined the military. Mark was already in high school when I was in pre-K, so of course we weren't close though we were first cousins. He's still overseas somewhere. Once he left, he never really came back and barely kept in touch. So it was just the three of us after that." She turned to face him. "My mother died when I was four. Brain tumor."

At a loss for words, Luke simply brought her hand to his mouth and kissed it.

"My Dad never really got over it...got over her. He was depressed for a long time, but he worked hard to give me everything I needed and wanted. His only request was for me to be smart, to stay focused and to make something of myself."

"I'm sure he's proud of you," he added. "Especially now that you're on your way to Hollywood."

"Actually, I haven't told him. With the wedding and everything, I figured he should just focus on that and his new life with Celeste. She makes him happy." Abruptly pushing herself off the ground, she stood and stretched before looking down at him. "We should get back...I don't want your family thinking I've kidnapped you or something. I can tell they've missed you, especially Lizzie. I think I finally won her over though. She grilled the hell out of me."

"She did what?" Luke asked as he stood to his feet.

"Oh yeah...that little cousin of yours told me in no uncertain terms that she had to make sure I was good enough to be friends with her Uncle Luke." She looked over at him and grinned. "So I showed her some pictures of my work I have stored in my phone...and when she peeped my Anna and Elsa reincarnations, she gave me the cool stamp."

"Damn," he replied, guiding her back to the crowd and draping his arm over her shoulder again. "Lizzie doesn't give those out too often. I'm impressed."

"Hey, it *is* Halloween," she said, looking up at him. "I wonder if I can graduate from cool to awesome if I paint the kids' faces?"

"If you did that, I promise you would *rule...*"

Aris laughed at his impression of Izzie when he exaggerated the last word. "Then it looks like I've got work to do! But first, I need some tools. We've got about an hour before the art store closes. It's about twenty minutes from here."

"Then we'd better hurry up."

Luke and Aris made a quick run to the store and returned in time for her to paint all of the children's faces. Once she was done, Lizzie rounded up all of the adults to watch their impromptu catwalk showcase that she named *Aris's Wacky Designs*.

When the applause finally died down and all the digital photos were taken, Lizzie gave Aris an enthusiastic high-five, officially sealing her with the coveted awesome stamp.

Later in the evening, Luke and Aris said their goodbyes and started the drive back to their hotel in Hilton Head. They arrived an hour later, still wired from Luke's family gathering. As they strolled through the lobby, Aris's eyes caught the activity happening near the pool. She turned to him and started wiggling as a smile lit up her face. "Good times, right?"

"Right," he agreed. "Let's go."

~ 20 ~

When they stepped through the doors and back into the warm, night air, Aris led them to a couple of lounge chairs near the pool. They learned that the hotel staff closed this area off to kids after 8PM, so it was a completely adult situation, allowing everyone to enjoy themselves freely with no worries.

As Aris wandered off to claim two lounge chairs, Luke walked back to the hostess stand. Minutes later, he returned to see her dragging two small tables behind her.

"Check it out," she said, proud of her furniture arrangement. "We definitely needed these little tables for snacks and drinks. And I almost got jacked for these cushy loungers, but I had to have them...they're much better than those hard ones over there."

"This is great, Moody, but I've got something better."

Following his eyes, she noticed an empty cabana a

few yards away. "No way…"

"I convinced the hostess to let me have it for the rest of the night. The group who reserved it left the hotel and won't be back until tomorrow, so…"

"So you flirted shamelessly with the chick and stole it," she replied with a laugh. "Cool. Whatever works."

They settled into the cabana and enjoyed the sofa, minibar and flat panel television though they spent most of their time just people watching. Eventually, they found their way to the edge of the infinity hot tub and submerged their feet and legs in the water while talking and taking shots with locals and visitors. Everyone kept mistaking them for a couple, but Aris didn't mind at all. Nor did she mind the way Luke's hands continually made contact with her body and his lips found her face and shoulders at every opportunity.

Feeling feverish, she blamed it on the shots and the steamy water. Luke stared at her off and on for several minutes before finally asking if she was ready to call it a night. Nodding, she followed him back to his suite and told him goodnight as soon as he slid the chain in place on the door. She had every intention of going into the bathroom alone, but somehow they ended up tangled and panting on top of the counter…

Slipping and sliding in the shower…

Banging and moaning against the bedroom wall…

And then tonguing and grinding in bed.

Aris couldn't believe how effortlessly her body responded every time Luke touched her, kissed her, stroked her…as if he alone controlled the rise and fall of her tides.

No man had been able to do that for her before.

Ever.

His hands gripped her waist as she rotated her hips and tightened around him. She was straddling him, his back flush against the headboard, his mouth fastened on her nipple. When she leaned back, he looked up at her and stared into her eyes...and then, for a brief moment, she lost her rhythm, her confidence...

It's in your nature.

You'll never be right for him.

When she looked away, he reached up and turned her head toward him until they locked eyes again. She was frozen, having stopped all movement, her heart beating erratically inside her chest.

How could you ever satisfy a man like him?

He grabbed her ass, holding her in place as he thrust into her, making her moan, bringing her back until her eyes closed and she slowly found her rhythm again.

Dipping her head, she kissed him passionately.

He isn't yours.

Angered and crushed by that truth, her eyes flew open and she anxiously shifted and fell back against the bed, pulling him with her until he was on top, her legs securing him, trapping him as their mouths danced. When he tried to slow their pace, she became more frantic, her movements wild and jerky. Pulling back, he stopped mid-stroke and gently grabbed her wrists before pinning them above her head.

"Relax, baby..." He watched her intently as he began to move again, inching deeper and deeper. He stroked her slowly, deliberately, until the creases between her eyes disappeared. "Stop thinking. Let me love you."

He lowered his head, chanting the last four words in

her ear as he made love to her, over and over again, until she exploded and he gritted his teeth and moaned her name, waves of pleasure rippling through them both as they tumbled over the cliff together.

~ 21 ~

NOVEMBER

Shortly before dawn, Luke opened his eyes.

The bed was empty, a written note resting in the place where Aris's head should have been.

Tossing the note, sheet and blanket aside, he grabbed a pair of cargo pants and a shirt from his suitcase before entering the bathroom to freshen up. After leaving the suite, he caught the elevator, rushed through the lobby and out to the patio and gardens that led to the beach where he spotted a lone figure standing in the distance near the water's edge.

Luke quietly entered Aris's space and sat in the sand a few feet away from her, watching as she took a step forward, the tide kissing her toes as it ebbed and flowed. He dropped his head and curbed his urge to chide her about leaving him early morning notes on pillows and wandering out onto the beach in the dark by herself, knowing that the danger of her decision wasn't lost on her...just like she'd already known that he would read her message when he woke and eventually join her so she wouldn't be alone.

He looked up to see her glancing over her shoulder at him, aware of his presence before he could say one word. Her grin revealed that he hadn't startled her at all, that she had expected to turn and see him there.

That made him smile.

When she shifted her eyes back to the water, his chest tightened as he realized how much he wanted to always be there for her, wherever and whenever she needed him.

Minutes later, the sun peered over the water. He watched as she wrapped her arms around her body, taking in the magnificent blends of red, orange and yellow as the sun rose and cast its beauty over the ocean. Glancing over her shoulder again, she blessed him with a bright smile that reached her eyes. He nodded, acknowledging the beauty of the moment and how fortunate he felt to share it with her, to see the pure delight on her face as she lifted her gaze and looked at the sky.

Luke continued to stare, the melodic sound of Aris's laughter lifting the weight of his worry. When she began to kick her feet and dance in the waves, he smiled again, relieved to know that—despite the fear and confusion he'd seen in her eyes as they further blurred the lines of their friendship just hours ago—at least for now, in this moment, she seemed...happy.

"I love this," she finally said, looking out over the ocean to the horizon. "So beautiful."

He nodded again, still watching her.
Marveling at how beautiful and fragile she truly was.

~ 22 ~

Standing on the balcony, Luke checked his watch for the fifth time. The wedding was due to begin in half an hour, but Aris had not yet emerged from the bedroom. After finishing his shower, he had grabbed his clothing and left the bedroom to give her space. To think. To breathe. She hadn't spoken since they'd left the beach and even then she hadn't said more than a few words. Her distance disturbed him and, for the first time since they'd met, it felt like she was in a place where he wouldn't be able to reach her. Frustrated, he just hoped that his presence would be enough to get her through what he was sure would be a difficult day.

Rubbing his head, he stepped back into the suite just as the door to the bedroom opened. A moment later, Aris glided out and faced him.

Sometimes he often forgot that she was a licensed esthetician who specialized in beauty and makeup, an art with a keen eye for color and style. He'd grown to love the simplicity of her look—a flawless complexion without enhancements, her skin naturally aglow and always soft and smooth to the touch. Yet, as pretty as she was, he sometimes wondered just how gorgeous she would look transformed. He'd seen a hint of it the night she wore that black dress he now loved, but he was still curious what full-on glitz and glamour would look like on her...

But never in his wildest dreams could he have possibly imagined the vision who was standing before him...she was stunning.

"Too much makeup?" she finally asked, a hint of uncertainly in her voice. "Luke?"

"Huh? Uh, no...it's...you're perfect."

Blushing, she walked over to stand in front of him. "Well, I expected you to steal the show so I was just trying to keep up...I couldn't have you looking better than me."

She smiled at him, gloss shimmering on her berry-stained lips. A sweet, clean fragrance teased his nose, and it was all he could not to touch her. Kiss her. Mess up everything that she'd spent the past hour pulling together so she would look so amazing right now.

"Not possible." He extended his arm. "Ready?"

After a deep breath, she nodded. "I gotta be."

"I got you, Moody...you know that, right?"

Her smile returned, and his heart swelled. "I know."

When they arrived, Luke helped her out of the car and guided her through the hotel lobby. With every step, he could feel her smile slipping along with her resolve. They made to the gardens of the property just before the music began to play. Luke held her hand as they approached the designated sections for guests, wanting to ask why she hadn't proceeded to the front rows reserved for family but decided to let it go when she quickly pulled him into an empty middle row on the groom's side.

The processional was rather short, beginning with an elderly woman who he assumed was the mother of the bride followed by another woman, stylishly dressed in a graceful, floor-length, champagne-colored dress. She glided by, eyes facing forward, and he felt Aris's eyes on him as he watched the woman take a seat on the front row of their section.

Luke glanced at Aris, raising an eyebrow.

"My Aunt Laurene," she whispered in his ear before returning her attention to the handful of bridesmaids and groomsmen walking down the aisle.

He waited for her to share another name with him, but she didn't utter another word as the wedding party took their places on either side of the small gazebo.

When the groom finally appeared and stood in position, Luke's eyes shifted to catch the sweet smile on Aris's face that vanished as quickly as it appeared. He eased closer to her, and she pressed her body into his, giving his hand a gentle squeeze.

Moments later, the bride appeared with an elderly man by her side, identified as her father. The two shared a loving embrace before proceeding down the aisle, both smiling ear-to-ear. When they passed, Luke felt Aris's hand squeeze his again.

Once the officiant asked the guests to be seated, he began the ceremony and ended it twenty minutes later.

The newlyweds jumped a decorative broom and were presented as Mr. and Mrs. Anthony Collier.

As they proceeded down the aisle, the newlyweds smiled and waved at their standing guests with enthusiasm. Luke was thrown when they waved and smiled at Aris as if she were just another guest in the crowd. From what he understood, Aris hadn't seen her father in almost two years...and that was the greeting he had for his only daughter after getting married? A generic smile and wave?

Luke hadn't realized that his body tensed until Aris gently squeezed his hand again. The sight of the barely-there smile plastered on her face made his jaw clench. They stood quietly and watched the remainder of the wedding party and several guests follow the couple across the lawn and inside what appeared to be a clubhouse adjacent to the hotel's conference center.

As they joined the crowd, Luke thought it odd that very few guests acknowledged Aris and the few that did seemed surprised to see her. When they entered the foyer of the clubhouse, she signed the guest book and then turned to tell him that she needed to stop by the restroom. Deciding to do the same, he followed her and ducked into the men's room, strolling out a short while later to wait for Aris in a nearby corner.

The woman in the champagne-colored dress — Aunt Laurene — was fluttering about the foyer, laughing and blowing air-kisses to everyone within her reach. Her eyes raked over him briefly before she was distracted by more guests who triggered another round of laughs, air-kisses and hugs.

When Aris emerged from the restroom, she found

him immediately. Aunt Laurene's eyes shifted to Aris, her face producing a curious expression before she began walking in their direction. As Aris got closer, Luke tilted his head in her aunt's direction and Aris nodded with a small smile, grateful for the heads up but seemingly aware that she'd already been spotted.

"Aris?"

She faced her aunt with a grin, still manufactured but a much better effort from earlier during the ceremony. "Hi, Aunt Laurene. How have you been?"

"I'm very well," she replied, her eyes now raking over Aris. "I must say...I'm surprised to see you."

As if suddenly remembering that they were related, Aunt Laurene reached in for a hug that held all the warmth of a southern blizzard.

"Does your father know you're here?"

Blinking, Aris didn't respond.

"I suppose he saw you in the crowd. They're taking pictures now, but I'm sure he'll find you soon."

Luke tensed again, but he felt Aris's hand slip into his and give him yet another squeeze.

"They know I'm here," Aris said, fully recovered. "I saw them both. It was a lovely ceremony, wasn't it?"

"Indeed, it was. Thanks to me." Aunt Laurene laughed, placing a hand over her pearls. "It was no easy feat. That Celeste is quite an interesting woman, but she finally came around to my suggestions. Lucky for her, event planning is my specialty!"

"Yes, Aunt Laurene...you've always known how to throw a spectacular bash." Turning to Luke, Aris revealed her first genuine smile since they'd arrived at the hotel. "This is my friend, Luke Donovan. Luke, this is my father's sister, Laurene Collier."

Extending his hand, Luke presented a smile as fake as the one Aris wore earlier. "Hello, Ms. Collier. This is quite an event."

Aunt Laurene smiled warmly as she covered his hand with both of hers. "Why, thank you. Such an attractive and distinguished young man you are. I'm surprised you're here with this niece of mine. Tell me...how *did* you two meet?"

"We live in the same neighborhood," Aris replied quickly. "If you'll excuse us, Aunt Laurene...we're going to find our seats."

"Celeste saved a place for you at the family table. I'm sure we can find an available space as well for your... friend." Aunt Laurene smiled at Luke again before turning a cool gaze to Aris. "Celeste insisted that you wouldn't miss such a special day the way you do most other important occasions. To be honest, I wasn't so sure that you'd show." She raised a brow. "You *are* still planning to sing...aren't you?"

Luke paused at that announcement, his eyes wide as he turned to stare at Aris.

Grinning, Aunt Laurene turned her attention to Luke. "I take it you've never heard Aris sing before?"

Still staring, he watched as Aris looked down at her hands, shifting uncomfortably under his gaze.

She could sing?

A small smile touched his lips as his interest piqued, similar to the way it had the first time he entered her apartment and discovered her mannequins. Just when he thought he knew all there was to know about her, he found more. It intrigued him as much now as it did that night, reminding him how much he wanted to know everything about her.

Because it mattered to him.

She mattered to him.

"Her voice is magnificent," Aunt Laurene added. "She gets it from her mother." She turned toward a guest standing behind her. "If you'll excuse me."

After her aunt dismissed them, Luke led Aris into the ballroom and found their table. Though he had a dozen questions, he sensed that she needed some time alone, so he kissed her forehead and went in search of beverages. Something strong, preferably bourbon.

Arriving at the table five minutes later, he held a whiskey sour in one hand and a white wine in the other. "Take your pick."

Of course, she went for the bourbon and he laughed as she downed half the glass in one gulp. Glancing up at him, she grinned but it didn't lessen the worried expression on her face. "Thanks...for everything."

He pressed his lips against her forehead again and sat beside her. Her aunt and a few other guests joined them and the band began playing. After the wedding party entered the ballroom and settled behind the head table, Aris stood to her feet. Before he could ask if she was all right, she gave him a weak smile and walked toward the stage to join the band. As the emcee hyped the crowd, she huddled with the musicians. Nodding her head, she turned to face the audience but the guy at the keyboard waved her back over for more discussion. She said a few words and they all nodded in agreement before she stepped away to position herself behind the microphone stand

Her father stood at the edge of the dance floor, staring adoringly at his new wife who was the center of attention as she smiled and laughed in her father's arms, already slowly swaying as they waited for the music to fill the ballroom.

Luke ignored all the *oohs* and *ahhs* they generated, his gaze on Aris though she didn't know it because her eyes were fixated on her father.

As the first chords of the guitar were played, he watched her take a deep breath. She looked down for a brief moment before peering out into the audience, her eyes shifting to the edge of the dance floor where her father stood, still enraptured by his new wife.

Luke's brows creased, his heart breaking for her as she sang about the love between father and daughter, her pain coming through every word, as if she was singing just for Tony, almost willing him to shift his eyes her way for just one fleeting moment.

But her father never noticed.

He was focused only on Celeste.

As the song came to an end, the crowd burst into enthusiastic applause for the touching dance as well as for Aris's beautiful delivery. Aunt Laurene reached out and touched his arm, a satisfied look on her face. "See...I told you her voice is incredible."

Luke nodded absently, wondering how everyone in the room could be so completely oblivious to what he'd just witnessed. "Yes...she is."

Watching her carefully, he finally caught her eyes.

She mouthed two words. "I'm okay."

The sadness on her face made his hands clench into fists. He stood to his feet, knowing that she was far from okay, but her assertive nod made him pause.

She held up one finger.

He'd forgotten she also had to sing the first dance.

As the words from *Golden* slipped through her lips, Luke's heart hammered in his chest as he sat down. It was unreal how expressive her voice was, how exquisite she was when she sang. He'd rarely seen such raw emotion from her except when he caused it... during those intimate moments like the one they shared last night.

As she sang about love and commitment, the desperation of the lyrics coming through loud and clear, he found that he wanted both for her more than anything...and he wanted to be the one to give her forever just as the song said.

With her eyes closed and her voice ringing in the air, she was so beautiful that tears stung his eyes.

And he wasn't the only one.

Missing a few steps as he danced with Celeste, Tony was mesmerized, his eyes locked on Aris as if he was seeing a ghost. Tears were welling up so fast that he looked away and abruptly left the ballroom, Celeste fast on his heels.

When the song was over, the audience erupted with praise for Aris, who stood like a statue. All the emotion and feeling she'd displayed were now gone, as if she'd turned inside herself, her eyes resembling those of the mannequins she painted.

Luke stood again, this time not caring if Aris wanted him to stay seated, but the band launched into another song, an up-tempo number that caused everyone to rush the dance floor, making it difficult for him to reach her before she fled the stage and slipped out of a side door.

Aris wandered out into the foyer and stopped when her father called her name.

"You're so much like her," Tony said when she faced him. "Your eyes, your voice, your…everything."

She stood quietly, observing him while he looked at her, looked through her, drifting back to a time gone by. Recognizing the familiar sorrow in his eyes, she stepped forward to kiss his cheek. "It's a celebration…a fresh start. No need to relive the past today."

"You're right," he replied, shaking his head. After an awkward pause, he opened his arms to her and attempted to smile. "It's a new day."

Stepping into his embrace, she rested her head against his chest.

"I wasn't sure if you were going to make it. Celeste told me that you had car trouble?"

"No worries," she replied. "I got here safely."

"You got it repaired on your own?" Surprise colored his tone. "Did you finally come to your senses about getting a real job that pays well?"

She stiffened in his arms.

"Okay, okay…it's a new day." He patted her back. "I'm just glad you could make it, honey bun. You sing even more beautifully than your mother did. She would be so proud of you." He angled his head to look down at her. "I'm proud of you too. You know that, right? You're my baby girl. I love you, Aris."

Grateful for the words she'd wanted to hear from him all day, Aris looked into her father's eyes and smiled. "I love you too. And I'm glad you found Celeste...I can tell she really makes you happy."

"She does," he said, his voice full of love for his bride. "The happiest I've been in a very long time."

Lifting his head to look behind her, Aris noticed his expression change. Tony's arms went slack as he continued to stare, so she turned in the direction of his gaze, curious to see what had caught his attention.

Luke.

"May I help you?" Tony looked down, noticing the smile on Aris's face. "Do you know this man, Aris?"

"He is my friend, Daddy," she replied on cue. "Luke Donovan. Luke, this is my father, Tony Collier."

"A friend?" Tony asked as he extended his hand to Luke in greeting. "Aris has never really had many of those; she's always been more of a loner. Yet, she brought *you* here." He regarded Luke with an equal measure of interest and suspicion. "You must be a pretty special friend to my daughter...Luke Donovan."

Luke shook and released his hand, holding his gaze the entire time. "She's very special to me, and I'm happy to be here with her."

"I see." Tony's eyes narrowed before he nodded and turned to Aris with a look of disappointment. "Is this how you were able to get here? Why didn't you just call and ask me for the money?" Without waiting for a response, he reached into his pocket and removed his wallet. Then, he counted out several large bills before presenting them to Luke. "I appreciate your generosity and ensuring that Aris made it here safely. This should cover her travel expenses for the weekend."

Aris quickly extended her arm to stop Luke when he took a step toward Tony. "No, I got here on my own. Luke is here as my guest."

Tony ignored her explanation and placed the cash in her hand instead, forcing her to keep it when she attempted to push back. Embarrassed, she launched into random chatter about beautiful the wedding turned out and where he and Celeste were planning to honeymoon while Luke listened in tense silence. After Aris exhausted her questions and ran out of things to say, Tony checked his watch, kissed her cheek and excused himself to check on Celeste.

"Enjoy your honeymoon," Aris called after him.

"Thanks, honey bun!" Tony waved as he rushed off. "I'll talk to you when we get back."

"Sorry about that. We can go now...if you're ready."

"You have nothing to apologize for," Luke replied, still pissed at what he'd just witnessed and the totality of the day. Placing a hand on her lower back, Luke guided Aris away from the boisterous laughter and music coming from the ballroom. He cursed under his breath, wondering how long it would be before anyone would even notice she was gone.

Soon, they were inside the rental car and cruising the short distance to their hotel. He held her hand the whole way while she sat quietly, staring out of the window.

Once they entered the suite, she headed straight into the bathroom, shutting the door behind her. Cursing again, he pulled off his suit jacket, loosened his tie, ran a hand roughly over his head and paced the room until he heard a loud noise.

"Aris?"

No response.

"Aris!"

He rushed to the bathroom, testing the door. Grateful that it was unlocked, he pushed it open and stopped short when he saw her on the floor, tears streaming down her face.

"I'm sorry...these damn heels. I fell." She pulled the back of her hand across her face, smearing mascara across her cheek. "I'm just so clumsy...I'm okay. I fell." She looked away. "I fell...I fell..."

Sinking to the floor, Luke pulled her into his arms as she finally fell apart.

~ 23 ~

She was warm and comfortable. Music was playing.

Opening her eyes, Aris flinched against the brightness of the room, the light flooding through the open doors to the balcony. Strong arms flexed as they tightened their hold about her body, her head pressed against a smooth, naked chest, slowing rising and falling, a heartbeat in her ear.

Luke.

Aris was flush against his side, her legs entwined with his. She blinked a few times, pressing her lips together just before she felt him hug her again and kiss the top of her head.

"Hey, Moody," he finally said, his voice rumbling through his chest against her ear. "You woke up just in time. Look what's on."

Lifting her head to peek above the covers at the television, she saw Harry Connick Junior and Sandra

Bullock spinning around in each other's arms, dancing.

Aris hadn't realized that Luke's hand was buried in her messy hair until his fingers began to move, massaging her scalp. It felt good.

"You're right, Moody," he said, kissing the top of her head again. "This is a pretty good movie."

She nodded, his heartbeat still in her ear as she continued watching *Hope Floats*, secure in his arms until the credits rolled and she drifted back into a deep, peaceful sleep.

~ 24 ~

Careful not to disturb Aris, Luke grabbed the open beer sitting on the nightstand and took a swig. She'd slept most of the day, tucked next to him. When she was awake, she barely spoke and ate very little food.

Though he was still worried about her, he let her rest and kept himself entertained watching football all afternoon, only leaving her side to take a trip to the bathroom and to accept food deliveries from room service throughout the day.

She finally stirred against him as the sun was setting, surprising him with a request to hang out for the night. When he asked what she wanted to do, she shrugged her shoulders and disappeared into the shower. By the time she was clean and dry, he'd already made a room reservation at a hotel near the riverfront in Savannah. There was more to do in the city, and it just made sense to stay there overnight. Less of a drive to the airport in the morning.

A few hours later, they were tucked away in a corner booth of a trendy bar in the heart of Savannah's historic district, eating hot wings, taking shots and listening to live music. They eventually returned to the hotel and camped out on the balcony, laughing and talking until they ran out of words. There was no sex when they finally made it to bed. Instead, he just held her like he'd done most of the day, listening to her soft snores until he finally drifted off to sleep.

Later that morning, they awoke in a slight panic after having overslept. Glancing at his phone, he realized it must have died while they were at the bar the night before. He chuckled to himself, trying to remember the last time he had actually forgotten to charge or check his phone. Definitely a first. After plugging the charger into the wall, he connected the cord to his phone and joined Aris in her rush to get dressed and check out so they wouldn't miss their flight back to Dallas.

Lucky for them, they were able to turn in their rental car and make it to the gate with a few minutes to spare. Finally seated with his seatbelt fastened, he relaxed and closed his eyes for a moment. Feeling her lips on his cheek, he cracked a lid and smiled at her.

"Thank you again, Luke Donovan," she said sincerely, returning his smile. "For everything."

He lifted her hand to his lips and kissed it.

She fell asleep during the flight, her head on his shoulder while he used his tablet to get caught up on the latest news. As the plane began its descent, he did his best to ward off the dread he was beginning to feel. There were dozens of messages on his voicemail to return, not to mention the pile of work he had waiting for him. More than that, he wasn't ready for his time with Aris to end. This trip was supposed to nix his infatuation, but the opposite happened.

He was going to miss the hell out of her.

That thought stayed with him as they walked through the airport to the parking area. Noticing she was a bit quiet herself, he threaded his fingers through hers as soon as they were inside his car. He could already feel her drifting away to that place where she couldn't be reached. But he had no idea what to say. Savannah was more than either of them had bargained for, their relationship now twice as complicated now than before they'd left.

After a tense and silent ride, he pulled into her driveway and cut the engine. "You don't have to be alone right now." He glanced at her, waiting for her to look at him. "I can stay—"

"I'm fine," she replied, squeezing his hand before letting it go. "I promise."

A part of him wanted to insist, but he pressed his lips together and nodded instead. He opened the door and climbed out, barely able to manage the surge of emotion tightening his chest as he made his way around the car to open her door. She looked up at him and smiled, but it didn't disguise the lost look in her eyes. Closing the door, he opened his mouth to tell her he was staying but an approaching car caught his attention. It came to an abrupt stop, blocking the driveway, and the driver jumped out, a scowl on her face as she stormed toward them.

"I guess this explains why you haven't returned my

calls," Jessica said nastily as her eyes shot daggers at Aris. "You've been *busy*."

"Jessica—"

"Were you really in Savannah with your family or were you with this bitch the whole time?"

Feeling Aris tense against him, Luke stepped forward just as Jessica got directly in his face. "Calm down. We can talk about this later—"

"We will talk about this *right now*," Jessica yelled. She was seething. "Who is she?"

"A friend." He ran a hand roughly over his head in frustration. "You deserve an explanation, but first you need to calm down."

Jessica's eyes flashed in anger before they settled on Aris, who was walking toward her apartment. Before he could blink, Jessica took off in her direction. When Aris didn't respond to her taunts, Jessica got even more enraged and pushed her from behind. Stumbling, Aris paused and continued her retreat without turning around but Jessica stepped in her face, insults spewing from her mouth as she pushed Aris again, spoiling for a fight.

Luke grabbed Jessica's arm just as he heard Aris apologize. Furious, he pulled Jessica back toward her car and told Aris to go inside. But the minute he released Jessica's arm, she slipped away and made her way back to Aris, attacking her again. Only this time, Aris exploded, knocking Jessica to the ground.

He rushed to grab Aris and secured her arms to keep her from swinging again, but the damage was done. She was still struggling against him when Jessica sat up and placed a hand against her bloodied lip.

"Stop it, Moody! It's me. It's me...calm down!"

He turned Aris to face him and she looked dazed. When she finally focused on his face, she turned to look at Jessica and then down at her hands, tears welling up in her eyes. "I'm sorry."

Jessica tried to get up and go after her again, but Aris ran into her apartment and slammed the door.

Luke finally looked at Jessica, anger distorting his face. "Go. Now."

When he made no attempt to follow her to her car, Jessica's eyes widened. "You're staying here with *her*? Are you fucking kidding me right now? After all I've done for you? If it wasn't for me, your ass would still be buried under a mountain of student loans trying to find a damn job—"

Unable to tolerate her mouth any longer, he approached her with rage in his eyes. He deserved her anger, but she'd gone way too far. Just as he was about to go off, he paused to really look at her. Her unkempt hair and attire, which had nothing to do with her altercation with Aris. Something was wrong. Even on her worst day, Jessica was immaculately groomed. Appearance was everything to her. Something was definitely wrong.

"Jess, what is this shit? What's going on with you?"

Still angered, Jessica dodged Luke's hand when he tried to grab her arm. "Fuck you. Your concern is a little too late."

"Jessica—"

She ran to her car, climbed inside and sped off.

Luke glanced at Aris's apartment, releasing a harsh breath. Frustrated, he pulled out his phone and dialed

Jessica. He wasn't surprised when she didn't answer. Scrolling through his voicemail, he played her messages from yesterday and his heart dropped.

Her father was in ICU. A massive heart attack.

No wonder she'd been disheveled. Her father was literally clinging to life and all her calls to him had been ignored. Worse than that, she'd found him with another woman.

He eyed his car, knowing he should go after Jessica...

But he turned and sprinted to Aris's apartment.

She'd left the door open, so he entered and shut it behind him, searching the room until he saw her sitting in the corner of the living room on the floor near her mannequins, her arms wrapped around her legs.

"Are you all right?" she asked, looking up at him. "I'm sorry. I always ruin everything. I'm so sorry."

"Don't apologize. That wasn't your fault."

"Is she still outside?"

He chuckled before he could stop himself. "I think she knew better than to come up here and get her ass kicked again."

A small smile touched her lips. "I didn't mean for that to happen. I—"

"She provoked you. Angry or not, Jessica had no right putting her hands on you." He pulled a hand down his face and sighed. "She's not herself right now. She's dealing with some things and—"

Aris held up her hand to stop his explanation. "You disappeared on her for days, and she found you with me. She has the right to be in her feelings. To fight for you...for what's hers." She paused and looked up at the ceiling. "I get it."

As he stared at her, guilt surfaced. Imagining Mr. Knox in the hospital, what that had done to Jessica, to her family...and he hadn't been there for any of them.

Luke looked away. "It's complicated."

"Isn't it always?"

Her tone was surprisingly light. He caught her eyes and she flashed a barely-there grin as she shrugged and scrambled to her feet. He told her to lock up and she nodded, closing the door behind him, already slipping into the place he could never reach her before the locks slid into place.

~ 25 ~

Luke eased his car into Jessica's driveway and called her again. No answer. He tried a few more times before giving up. If she didn't want to talk, he understood that...but he needed to be sure that she was all right.

He approached her front door, sliding the key into the lock without bothering to knock first. Then, he disarmed the alarm and called her name. No answer.

After climbing the stairs, he found her in bed. She looked even worse than when he saw her earlier, and the sight made his throat close. Despite their problems, despite his confusion about Aris and what he'd allowed himself to do over the weekend, Luke loved Jessica. Knowing that she was hurting, the only place he knew to be was by her side.

Jessica heard him enter the room, but she remained on her side with her back to the door. He climbed into bed and wrapped his arm around her waist, pulling her close. When she began to cry, he kissed the back of her shoulder.

"Who is she, Luke?"

Luke closed his eyes, unsure of how he should answer the question. He owed her the truth, but he wasn't ready to hear it himself. "She's a friend."

It sounded lame to his own ears, but he didn't dare say more.

"Did you sleep with her?"

He flinched at her question, at the catch in her voice. For a moment, he had to think back to the last time he'd seen her cry. It was years ago, when her grandmother died. And though her father was currently clinging to life, Luke was certain that the pain in her voice right now was due to the deductions she'd made seeing him in a neighbor's driveway a day later than his scheduled arrival with another woman in his car.

He'd already made a fool of her once.

Lying to her now was not an option.

"Yes."

Jessica didn't move. The words covered them, adding yet another layer of problems...one that once seemed unimaginable.

They were Luke and Jessica.

They were the mold, the prototype.

There had never been a question of whether or not they would make it through every obstacle unscathed.

But here they were.

"I'm sorry, baby." Luke said, kissing her hair. "I'm so sorry about your father, about what I've done...for not being there when you needed me, for what you saw, for hurting you—"

"I forgive you."

Luke didn't notice he was holding his breath until Jessica finally turned to face him, her red-rimmed eyes searching his. Her hand came up to caress his face, and he closed his eyes to keep from looking at her. At that moment, he didn't deserve the love he saw in her eyes.

"I don't know how we got here, but we can't be *that* couple. I don't know who that woman is...was... but she's not me. She was just...easier than me right now. Like other men might seem easier than you at times. But we're better than easy...we're better than cheating and lying to each other. We're a team, Luke. We're *us*."

He caught her reference to Quincy, a rich boy that caught her eye back in grad school during one of their rough patches. The difference between then and now was Jessica had been up front with Luke about Quincy, recognizing the potential for trouble and immediately informing him about her attraction so they could shut it down. Together.

Luke felt her lips touch his, but he didn't respond right away. Jessica didn't let that or her earlier injury deter her because she was on a mission now...shifting into fix-it mode as she always did when things were awry, when she sensed the disconnect between them and assumed that sex would always resolve their differences and close the distance.

She was *managing* him.

"Is it too late?" she asked quietly, nipping at his lips. "Who is she, Luke? What is it about her?"

He looked away, wanting to escape the conversation but accepting that he still owed her the complete truth, no matter how difficult it was to hear. "She makes me smile."

Jessica let out a harsh laugh as she shook her head in disbelief, her calm demeanor finally giving way to justifiable anger. "And I don't?"

"I didn't say that."

"What else aren't you saying? I guess my consistent ability to make you scream and curl your toes isn't enough for you anymore either, huh? What? She does that better too?"

Luke stared at her, wanting to tell her it really wasn't enough anymore. That if she has spent just as much time focusing on connecting with who he really was and establishing real intimacy rather pushing for who her father wanted him to be and mastering new sexual positions then maybe he wouldn't have turned to Aris at all. But Luke didn't say that—he couldn't say that—because it wasn't fair to blame Jessica for his own shit and it was completely wrong to suggest that she was responsible for not protecting his heart and allowing another woman to enter the space in his mind reserved only for her.

That was entirely on him...and he'd failed.

So he searched for the best way to affirm that Jessica was, is and always would be enough for him. That he loved her and he was sorry. That he would choose her every day...

But she lashed out before he found the words.

"I seriously doubt *that*," she said, answering her own question. "So what is this? Some silly attempt to see if the grass is greener? That's beyond trite, Luke...even for you."

Luke twisted his mouth, watching her morph before his eyes. "And what if that was the reason?"

Jessica flipped her hand dismissively. "Then I expect you to just say that, and I could've given you a pass."

"A pass?"

"Yes, a pass," she replied, nastily. "Look, I get that we've been together a long time and you're probably... curious. You should have just said something. That way, we could have discussed it and I could have—"

"What?" Luke finally snapped. "Managed it like you do everything else in our relationship? What...you would have picked the chick too?"

"Well...yes." She sat up and tossed her head, chewing on her bottom lip as if staging a coup. "That way, it resolves your issue while keeping me involved. I suppose I could have arranged a threesome or something like that. Clearly, I should have...given the choice *you* made." She rolled her eyes. "That was probably the most insulting part of me having caught you today. I mean really, Luke...couldn't you have done better than her?"

And there it was. What it had always been.

She never respected his choices, his wants, his needs.

Jessica Knox always knew what was best.

He stood from the bed and crossed the room to look out of the window. "I think it's best we end this conversation."

Her eyes were on him. He could feel it. Still, he refused to look at her.

"All right, baby. We'll just pick this up later." Standing from the bed, she closed the distance between them and cupped his face in her hands. "Everything will be fine. We'll get through this...together."

Luke moved away from her and grabbed his keys off the nightstand.

Jessica blinked. "Where are you going?"

He paused, remembering the real reason he had come to see her. "I'm just going to run to the store real quick. Then, we can go see your father."

"Sounds good." She moved to her dresser and stared in the mirror, lighting touching her bruised lip. "Oh, and don't forget we have a business dinner later tonight with a new client. I'm wearing teal, so it would be great if you would wear your navy suit. I pushed our reservation back to 8 p.m. so we'll have enough time to change after leaving the hospital. It's at the steak house downtown—I know you love that place and we haven't been in a while. As a matter of fact, let me check to see what specialties Chef Marlo has planned for tonight."

Luke stood in the doorway as Jessica placed her phone to her ear and eventually launched into a lively conversation with the chef. He listened as she chatted briefly about her father's health and *oohed* and *ahhed* over the specialty dishes he was apparently preparing "for his favorite couple."

As he observed Jessica's theatrics, he wondered if it would always be that way with them—power struggles, endless appointments, conflicting schedules and strategic business dinners. At one point he'd been satisfied with that life—after all, it was how you made it to the top.

But now that he was there, he could see that the view wasn't so great.

~ 26 ~

Luke passed several stores as he cruised down the parkway. At every traffic light, he had to stop himself from calling Aris. She didn't deserve to be pulled into his mess and, despite the bullshit she was spitting before he left, Jessica didn't deserve infidelity.

As much as he hated to admit it, Jessica was right. They had always been better than cheating and lies. For his entire adult life, nothing and no one had ever come close to accessing the space in his heart and mind reserved for her. Jessica was the most beautiful, confident woman he'd ever met. She had always been too good for him, which sadly had been his type of woman since he started sneaking into girls' cots in kindergarten during naptime.

But it was his high school girlfriend, Skylar, who actually broke his heart and left him for some dude with more money and a better car. When he made it to college, there were dozens of Skylars but he swore them off...until he met Jessica Knox.

Luke heard of her often during freshman year, but they never crossed paths. He wasn't very social on campus, preferring to spend his time with Devin and their smaller circle of friends. Luke's main goal had been to not fuck up and lose his partial scholarship because it—besides his low-paying job—was the only way he could afford to be in school at all.

Later, it became more and more obvious who Jessica was...more specifically, who her father was...so Luke immediately redirected his energy to more accessible girls. But when Jessica Knox strutted into his sophomore Circuits class, he was gone. Not only was she brilliant but, surprisingly, her looks actually surpassed the hype that preceded her. Still, he remained aloof. Skylar had been enough to last a lifetime, plus he had much less to offer Jessica, so why bother? Content with the girl he was currently dating, he kept his attention where it belonged...until Jessica finally approached him.

Needless to say, Luke was flattered. Having her interest and attention alone was enough to draw envy and instantly increase his status. Still, Luke kept his distance, politely declining Jessica's social requests out of respect for his current relationship but, with all the rumors and speculation, he got dumped and found himself single again before the semester ended.

Luke kept to himself all the way to final exams, but eventually caved when Jessica asked him to study. He'd assumed that it would be a group effort, but when he showed up it was just Jessica sitting alone in the courtyard. He noticed that she was a bit jittery when he sat down and, halfway through the study session, she was fidgeting so much that he had to ask if she was all right. She took a deep breath, looked him in the eyes and said, "You're too damn fine. How am I supposed to focus when you look like *that*?"

After a brief silence, they both burst into laughter.

That summer, they both stayed on campus and spent as much time as they could together. Luke found her to be nothing like what he'd expected—she was honest and direct, with a quick wit and an infectious laugh. He couldn't help but want to be around her...and, not surprisingly, just *want* her.

Best of all, they established a genuine friendship that blossomed slowly and, by the start of their junior year, they were official. From that moment, there had been no secrets between them. With Jessica, Luke gained a mentor in her father and an exclusive opportunity to make all the right connections. With Luke, Jessica learned to relax and enjoy life more plus it solidified her position as the baddest chick on campus. By senior year, everyone had already predicted their uber-success with three babies and mini-mansions on both the east and west coasts. Jessica's father would go on to pay for graduate school for them both and they would intern at Knox Corp until they graduated and assumed corner-office positions.

Jessica had literally changed his life and now they were what everyone around them aspired to be. Together, they were driven and established. He became the man all Jessica's friends secretly wanted for themselves, and she literally became the game changer who rewrites the rules while still managing to be the type of woman that powerful men pursue and win for other men to envy.

Luke pulled into Jessica's driveway, admiring the landscaping she'd just had done. It was their home, the one he would move into once he proposed and they officially agreed to spend their lives together. He had actually thought it was a premature purchase, but Jessica insisted on making it happen given the style, price and location. It would have been silly to walk away from it, and she was right...even if they weren't quite ready for it. It was a perfect choice.

Luke remained in the car, staring at his future. He had more than any person deserved to ask for, but he couldn't ignore the emptiness saturating his spirit. Every day that passed, he was becoming a much different man, someone even he didn't recognize. A man who was a lot less concerned about power and influence, optics and authority...one who no longer cared to be envied and emulated.

None of that mattered anymore.

He wanted to be happy.

~ 27 ~

FEBRUARY

When the hell had she become such a weeper?

Aris wiped her face with the back of her hand, remembering a time when she was so self-actualized that nothing could break her, her resilience so solid that pain could never penetrate.

No tears. No fears. Only epicness.

Sure she was ten years old at the time but so what?

It happened. It was real. She was badass.

Fast forward to now and here she was…curled into a ball in the middle of her bed, surrounded by worn strips of written affirmations, her pillow wet with tears that she'd been silently shedding for the past hour.

Maybe she was simply homesick though that was entirely laughable. Dallas just happened to be a place she'd lived for the past two years. The city was no more a home to her than Charlotte, Nashville and New

Orleans had been, each place just somewhere to go to keep from returning to Savannah.

Leaving Chatham County had been her only goal after high school. She had dreams of exploring the west coast and would have left the moment she received her diploma, but her father insisted on higher education and in-state tuition resulting in Atlanta becoming her first great escape. Aris dutifully put in her four years and as soon as she crossed that stage to accept the degree she didn't want, she presented it to her father, hugged him goodbye and fled as far as her graduation money would take her.

Over the years, she embraced the freedom and solitude and never stayed anywhere long enough to become attached in any way or to matter to anyone. She hadn't cared about building a life or other long-term headaches. The present was about all she could handle, and she took it one day at a time.

Laughter and conversation filled the room on the other side of her bedroom door, but she continued to feign sleep. Preferring to be alone, she closed her eyes and took slow, even breaths in an attempt to relax, but the face that appeared in her mind triggered another sting in her eyes and fresh tears tumbled out again.

She missed Luke.

Every time she closed her eyes anymore, there he was. Some fond memory of the two of them spending time together or, like now, just a mental picture she'd unconsciously taken of him and stored away. It was maddening. She had never missed anyone in her entire life, but somehow she was always missing *him*.

The discovery of this debilitating condition came the

day she began the long drive to Los Angeles…alone.

Traveling alone was nothing new. She had done it many times before without even a hint of sadness or regret. Starting over was her thing. She was exceptional at moving on and not looking back…but this time was different. Since that day she left Cypress Lake — left Luke — she'd been forcing herself to fend off the funk, to revert back to her pre-Luke days where she was okay with herself and her life. Where the only thing that mattered was her money and her mannequins.

Her mind was on board with that, for the most part.

But her heart refused to cooperate.

Every day, she wanted to pick up the phone. To call Luke and hear his voice. No one she'd met since she arrived in L.A. had piqued her interest or cared to nickname her the way he'd done although the people outside her bedroom door were completely convinced that she had serious emo issues.

But they didn't know her. No one knew her.

Not the way Luke did.

She could call him now. He might even answer, but any conversation between them was pointless. Sure, they were still friends but not the kind that spent time watching movies or playing games or eating hot wings like they used to do. She stopped being the friend who would call and tell him that she received a call back from a casting agent right before Christmas about her video submission for the new *FleshFX* reality show where she could showcase and cultivate her talent. He was no longer the buddy who would laugh at how shocked she'd been when she got the job or freak out with her about the craziness of filming episodes with the cast and crew in between her classes and internship.

In the month since she'd been in L.A., her life was taking off by leaps and bounds. Everything was coming up Aris, but Luke had no idea because he wasn't across the street or just a call or text away. He was no longer the first person she would tell her good news. They weren't friends, they weren't close and the emptiness was consuming her.

And now she was a bona fide crier.

She had hoped that it was just a phase. That, slowly but surely, she would just stop having feelings at all. That it would become...easier.

She was still waiting for that to happen.

Fortunately for her, every day wasn't totally awful. Some mornings she woke up with a forced enthusiasm, focused on putting the past behind her and seizing the day. She was in the freaking City of Angels. The place where stars were born and dreams came true. Hell, she was living her dreams now. Today. How long had she wanted this? How long had she imagined working toward the one thing she loved most in this world?

And now she was here. It wasn't a dream anymore.

She just never imagined that she could ever love anything more than her art. That everything in her life would be so muted without Luke to share it with her.

She'd been trying to jump that hurdle by connecting more with her roommate. Deena was a California native whose love for make-up and the fantasy genre rivaled her own. Though they were polar opposites, the two got along great. While Aris preferred her spot on the sofa or on the floor creating new designs, Deena was super social and actively immersed herself in the Hollywood scene. Once Deena realized that it was hopeless to pressure Aris into having good times, she ventured out and made more friends to join in her escapades, resulting in lots of peace and quiet for Aris in between her weekday internship and late-evening classes. She would occasionally venture out on her own to shop or try a new restaurant, but the L.A. lifestyle didn't really suit her. Outside of the beaches, it was just another place she couldn't call home.

Sitting up, she wiped her eyes and took a deep breath. This "homesickness" was dumb.

She had work to do.

Climbing out of bed, she shuffled into the bathroom and took a long, super-hot shower. Once she was dressed, she looked in the mirror and half-smiled at her reflection, appreciating her efforts to look casual-glam. Only her puffy eyes revealed the truth. Maybe people would be too distracted by her new Hollywood hair to notice. She turned her head to check out her playful 'do, highlights and all. Though she'd been less than thrilled when the producers expressed the need to "change her look" for the show, she had to admit that she loved the results of her L.A. style.

Returning to her bed, she gathered all her affirmations and stuffed them back into the tattered yellow folder. When she stuck them back into the nightstand, her phone buzzed.

Kim's face was on the screen.

"Hey…you good?"

"Yeah," Kim replied, out of breath. "I'm boarding my

plane now. Are you still coming to pick me up?"

"Of course. When do you land?"

"At one fifty-five. I would get there sooner if I didn't have this out-of-the-way connection in Denver...that's what I get for wanting the cheap flight...hold on a sec, I'm at my seat."

Aris heard a bunch of rustling for a few minutes before Kim came back to the phone. "Okay. I'm all settled. Be there soon...can't wait to seee youuu!"

Aris laughed, her spirits slowly lifting. "Me too, chick. Have a safe flight!"

Hanging up the phone, she shook her head. In addition to Luke, her intent had been to cut ties with Kim as well but the woman was stubborn as hell and left messages damn near every day saying she would not be ignored or tossed aside. Kim was back to her old self, running her boutique and coaching her high-school squad, showing them in grand fashion how cheers and stunts were supposed to be done. After the first call came another and before Aris realized it, Kim was no longer the one initiating their conversations. Kim never mentioned the new balance between them; instead, she simply said that everyone needed someone and she would gladly stand in until Luke was back in the picture.

Aris had hung up on her that day.

Then she'd called Kim right back that next morning.

Basically, those were her days and nights. School, internship, studying and occasional doses of Kim. It kept her mind off Luke, and she was grateful for that.

Thinking of him never left her in a good place, so she did her best to pretend that Savannah never happened.

She needed to focus on her career, and he needed to focus on his life with Jessica. Anytime she felt herself about to call him, she would reference his last text in her phone as a reminder that it was all for the best.

"I'm sorry, Moody."

He'd sent that message right before Christmas.

And they hadn't spoken to each other since.

Not that she had any grand expectations of their friendship after she moved, but she at least thought that they were better than her having to find out about his pending nuptials via the life section's front page on *dallasnews.com*.

She had been looking for the write-up on Kim's squad that she promised to read. Kim had texted her a million times asking her if she'd seen it. A freaking link to the article would have helped but that was too much like right for Kim — she rather send her on a search.

But what Aris found was not the celebratory photograph of the recently-awarded, high-school cheerleaders — instead, she saw the smiling faces of two of the most stunning people in the metro-Dallas area.

All Aris could recall was how happy Luke looked.

It was a teaser article, speculating the status of the beloved couple as photographers snapped their picture as they escaped some place in the city that Aris hadn't even known existed. According to the article, a source close to the "stunning couple" revealed that they may have already gotten engaged New Year's Eve...the same day Luke had sent Aris a text claiming how much he missed her.

When she confronted him via text the next morning after a sleepless night, Luke's only reply had been his "I'm sorry" text. Not a phone call. A *text*...with a promise of an explanation that never came, which was exactly why she'd chosen to revert back to her pre-Luke days. Whether it already happened or was about to happen, Luke would be a married man soon and, at some point, the father of a bunch of kids. She didn't know for sure, but Luke seemed like the type. She could see him driving with a car seat in a new SUV or passed out on the sofa with a baby on his chest.

Soon, he would be an excellent husband and father, and she would be working on a movie set, doing work so fabulous that the Academy would be calling her with a nomination...as it should be.

Always forward.

Hiking her bag up on her shoulder and grabbing the handle of her overstuffed suitcase, she left her bedroom and walked by the small crowd camped out in the living room.

"Hey, girl," Deena said, grinning as she turned her way. "Want to watch yourself on TV before you go?"

Aris cringed. "Hell no. I'll pass."

As Deena and Leslie laughed, Zack, Joey and Danny began teasing her, insisting that Aris had finally crossed over to the dark side, joining all the other D-list divas who always claimed to have more important things to do than to sit with mere mortals and partake of their sheer awesomeness on screen. She tried to keep a straight face, but the guys were in rare form as they walked over and dropped to their knees before her, begging for autographs on their faces. Laughing, Aris shook her head and blessed them with a middle-finger salute as she made her way to the foyer.

"I'm out," she said, pulling the door closed behind her. "Catch y'all later."

She hadn't taken more than a few steps when the door opened and Deena approached her. "Hey...are you really okay? You've been holed up in your room since you got off work yesterday. I thought maybe you were sick or something."

"I'm fine," she replied, shrugging. "Just feeling a bit overwhelmed lately. It'll pass."

"Maybe not with your crazy ass schedule. Between school, the job and the show, you barely have a minute to breathe...you really gotta slow down girl before your body does it for you."

"I know...but really, I'm fine. These few days off to hang out with Kim will do wonders."

"I agree...it wouldn't hurt to toss in some room service and a massage while you're at it," Deena replied before giving her a hug. "Enjoy yourself, Aris. I mean it...*have fun*."

"I will. *I promise.*"

"You better," Deena said, narrowing her eyes in mock threat before disappearing into their apartment.

By the time Aris ducked inside of her car and started the ignition, she decided that Deena was right. She was doing way too much in the name of keeping her mind off her problems. Clearly that wasn't working out very well since she'd been balling her eyes out since she woke up this morning. Looking in the rearview mirror, she smiled at her reflection.

Fun was on the horizon.

Kim couldn't have chosen a better time to visit.

When she arrived at the airport, Aris parked and made her way inside to the nearest restaurant to complete an assignment for class before Kim's plane landed. She spent the next hour sitting at a corner table with her laptop, a couple of mini tacos, a slice of thin-crust pizza and a tall glass of bourbon-spiked lemonade as she bobbed her head to the music streaming through her earbuds. Once she finished her assignment, she packed up her belongings and checked her watch, surprised that more than an hour had passed with no word from Kim.

Yanking the earbuds out, she checked her phone and noticed a missed call and voicemail message.

Kim had missed her connection in Denver and wouldn't arrive for at least another three hours.

Shaking her head, Aris dropped cash on the table, grabbed her stuff and left the departure level for the parking garage with her phone in hand. On her way there, she was distracted by a cute t-shirt in one of the gift shops and stopped to check the price. It looked like something Kim would wear, but it cost too damn much so she left it on the rack and turned to leave the store...crashing right into another customer, knocking her phone from her grasp. Before she could apologize, the man bent down to pick it up from the carpeted floor.

"Thank you," she said when he placed it in her hand. After dropping it inside her bag, she shook her head and shrugged. "I'm clumsy."

"I'd say gorgeous is a more fitting description, but hey...your choice. Clumsy, it is." The man extended his hand. "I'm Devin."

"Aris," she replied, slipping her hand into his. "Nice to meet you."

When he didn't immediately let go of her hand, Aris smiled awkwardly and pulled away. She tucked a strand of hair behind her ear, suddenly uncomfortable underneath his gaze.

"Forgive me for staring," Devin replied as he tilted his head and grinned. "Aris, you said? You wouldn't happen to know a guy named Luke, would you? Luke Donovan?"

At the mention of Luke's name, Aris's eyes widened. "Luke? Ahh, yes...umm, he was my friend—uhh, we were...he was my neighbor when I lived in Dallas." She narrowed her eyes. "How do you know him?"

Instead of answering her question, Devin focused his attention to an area just above her head. Curious, she turned to see what caught his eye and her breath caught as she heard Devin chuckle and reply, "Damn...this world is small as hell, ain't it?"

~ 28 ~

Throwing caution to the wind, Luke stepped forward and embraced Aris in a tight hug. He didn't wait to see her expression or worry that she might not be as happy to see him as he was to see her. It didn't matter. He felt like a kid in a candy store, and she was the treat he'd been saving to buy for months. When he pulled away, he was relieved to see her smiling back at him. After a brief pause, she said his name in wonder and he hugged her again, this time lifting her off the ground. Devin stood to the side, laughing his ass off, but Luke didn't care one bit.

He'd missed the hell out of her.

"I can't believe I'm actually looking at you right now," Aris said happily. "What are you doing here?"

"Business travel. Got a client presentation tomorrow morning and a few meetings after that." Luke couldn't help letting his eyes wander over her. "You look good,

Moody. New hair and everything."

She struck a playful pose. "My Cali vibe…like it?"

"I love it."

He hadn't meant for that truth to sound so intimate, but what was the point in pretending? She was still the same Aris, effortlessly pretty and donned in an off-the-shoulder top and jean skirt, but he still couldn't get over her hair…and the urge to bury his hands in it. Realizing that he was staring, he took a step back and placed his hands in his pockets.

Devin cleared his throat, still chuckling at their reunion. "Aris, we were on our way to grab something to eat. You're welcome to join us if you want."

Aris turned to Luke, searching his eyes. "I probably shouldn't. Plus, Kim's flying in, so I need to stick around here anyway and get some studying done…"

"Come on." Luke smiled, gesturing his head toward Devin. "He's harmless."

Aris looked away. For a moment, Luke was afraid she was going to say no but then she shifted her gaze back to him and smiled.

"Sure, I'll join you," she said. "As long as it's not too far from here. I have to get back in time to pick up a friend."

"Who?" Luke asked, searching her eyes.

Aris smirked at his sudden attitude. "Kim."

"Cool." He visibly relaxed and raised a brow. "When does her plane land?"

"She missed her connection and said it would be at least a few hours before she gets here."

"I'll be sure you make it back here by then." Luke reached over and relieved her of the laptop bag on her shoulder, placing it on top of his rolling suitcase. "Come on...we've got to go pick up our rental cars."

She hesitated. "While y'all do that, I'll go get my car. That way I won't have to pay all that unnecessary money to leave it parked here." She smiled. "I can meet you. Just text me where y'all decide to eat."

After a brief pause, Luke nodded and returned her laptop bag. "All right."

Hiking her bag onto her shoulder again, Aris turned on her heel and walked in the opposite direction.

A tavern with pub grub and music was the restaurant of choice. Once Luke and Devin finally arrived, the hostess seated them with Aris in a booth where they remained for the next two hours. Aris was in stitches from the guy's crazy stories during their college days, and Devin was fascinated by her work as they discussed cinema and special effects. There were several times when she would catch Luke staring at her after some goofy exchange or round of laughter, and she'd just smile and place a hand on his knee or against his cheek, so happy to have him close to her again.

"All right, I'm out of here for real this time. I told y'all I have to study." She tapped Luke's leg to get him to move so she could slide out of the booth. When she was on her feet, she extended a hand to Devin. "It was great meeting you."

"What's with the hand?" Devin asked, sliding out of the other side to stand and pull her into a hug. "You're fam now…give it up!"

Stepping away, Devin slipped back into the booth and announced that he had a phone call to make and would meet them outside after he took care of the bill.

"Where'd you park?" Luke asked once they were standing on the sidewalk outside the restaurant. His eyes scanned the busy street before resting on Aris. He smiled, happy to finally have her to himself.

"Not far. I got a good space. Good thing I didn't park at one of the meters." She checked her phone. "Kim should be here in another hour. Poor thing…she's had an awful travel day."

"Come on. I'll walk you."

The evening was warm and breezy as they slowly strolled along the sidewalk. They fell into step together but no words were exchanged. When Luke continued walking past her car, she looked up at him. "My car is right here."

"You're dying to get rid of me, huh?"

"I just thought Devin was waiting on you—"

"I'm with you right now. Devin can take care of himself." He grinned. "You okay with that?"

She slipped her hand in his and let him lead her to his rental car a block away. When she was settled inside the car, she caught herself smiling again.

"So how have you been…really?" he finally asked, brushing a strand of hair from her face.

"I've been okay. L.A. life is different, but I'm getting used to living here. My Dad and Celeste actually came out to visit me a couple of weeks ago if you can believe that…of course, it was Celeste's idea. Dad and I talk a lot more now, and it's nice. He's still pretty judgy about everything I've got going on, but that's just him." Shrugging, she smiled. "I'm okay with that."

He returned her smile, still playing with her hair.

"Let's see, what else is happening...well, I'm working my ass off every day, but I love it. My internship is the best, but it doesn't pay worth a damn. It's expensive living out here, so I'm on a serious budget. Like a-bowl-of-cereal-every-day-of-the-week type of budget." She grinned, her eyes softening as she stared at him. "Good thing I decided to treat myself today, or I would've missed you."

Unable to hold back any longer, he leaned in and kissed her. She still tasted like the strawberry shortcake they'd shared an hour ago and also like...Aris. Sliding closer, he buried his hands in her hair as he'd been wanting to do all evening, relishing her sighs.

"Damn, you make me dizzy," he said, nipping at her bottom lip. "I love kissing you..."

They stayed that way, lip-locked until his phone began to buzz. They ignored it at first, but when the buzzing stopped and then started up again a moment later, he reluctantly pulled away. After removing it from the case on his hip, he checked the voicemail message and cursed under his breath.

"Is everything okay? Was that Devin?" Aris asked, placing a hand on this arm. When he didn't respond right away, she pressed her lips together and trained her eyes on the lamp posts shining in the distance. "Jessica, right? Is she here?"

"She just got here." He sighed heavily. "I...she wasn't supposed to fly in until tomorrow night...her schedule must have freed up and she decided to join us for our demo in the morning —"

"I see," she said quietly, still unable to look at him. "So, you're kissing me now because...what? Seemed like a good time for you to take advantage of your temporary freedom before she popped up?

"No, it's not like that —"

"Then tell me," she said as she turned to glare at him when he tried to reach for her. "What *is* it like?"

He didn't respond.

The look on her face made his heart drop.

"The only reason you're here with me now is because your friend, Devin, just happened to bump into me." She laughed without humor. "You've known all along I was here in L.A. My number hasn't changed either. You had no intention of even saying hello while you were in town, did you?"

He toyed with the phone in his hands. "I wasn't sure if you'd even want to see me."

"How would you know that? You didn't even bother to call and find out." She snatched her bag from the floor of the car and reached for the door handle. "I have to go."

"Moody...wait!"

"For what?" Her eyes narrowed to slits. "What are you really doing right now with me, Luke? Do you even know?" When he didn't respond, she looked down and shook her head. "You don't want me. You just want something that's not already pre-scheduled, arranged and signed off on by Jessica." Lifting her head, she glared at him again. "I bet you're just hoping that I'll look on the bright side, huh? Like I don't know any better...like I don't know that once the thrill is gone, you'll run back to—"

"Moody, listen—"

"No, *you* listen," she replied, catching his eyes. "I've been a lot of things in my life but never this. This is not who I want to be. And what I *don't* need is a fake friendship with a guy who sees me as nothing more than an indulgent fantasy, like I'm some kind of to-do item you mark off your bachelor list before you can fully commit to your privileged life. I'm not a toy. You don't get to waste my time because you're not ready to face your fabulous future as Mr. Jessica Knox."

His jaw clenched. "You know good and damn well that is not what's happening here, Moody."

"Isn't it?" She laughed, crossing her arms over her chest in mock amusement though her eyes were clearly judging him. "Eventually you'll get past your commitment issues and return to your regularly-scheduled life and when that happens…then what? Huh? What happens to me?"

Frustrated by the truth in her words, he dropped his head in his hands. "You're speaking like our story's already written."

"Perhaps it is," she replied, opening the door. "I'm gonna go…take care of yourself."

"Moody…Moody!"

He pushed his door open and climbed out to go after her. Luke called Aris's name again, but she didn't turn around and continued walking. Everything she'd said had been wrong, and he was pissed. Did she really believe that she was nothing more than a distraction for him? He stopped abruptly and cursed, pulling a hand roughly down his face when he saw her cross the street in a rush to get even further away from him.

Cursing again, he turned away and walked back to his car where he noticed Devin opening the door to his own rental parked in front of Luke's.

"Where's Aris?" At the look on his friend's face, Devin shook his head. "What you do, man?"

"Not now," Luke said angrily as he threw himself inside his car, slamming the door closed.

~ 29 ~

MARCH

"Cheers to Aris," Deena yelled. "And cheers to the fuckin' weekend!"

Raising their shot glasses in the air, everyone toasted to the end of Aris's reality show run, screaming cheers before consuming their spirits. After hosting a viewing party for her elimination episode in their apartment, Deena invited everyone to the "official after party" at the neighborhood pub which was quickly becoming their favorite hangout.

Aris slammed the tiny glass on the counter and picked up the one right next to it, tossing it back and letting it burn its way down her throat. When her eyes refocused, she felt Deena and Leslie wrap their arms around her while Danny ordering another round along with some nachos, eggrolls, hot wings, chicken tenders and fries.

"Congrats again, Aris," Joey said as he walked over to join their group hug.

Leslie jumped in surprise before glaring at Joey. "Get your hand off my ass, J."

"Forgive me, love," he said without an ounce of sincerity. "I'm drunk."

Leslie rolled her eyes and excused herself to use the restroom just as Zach approached them, laughing at what he just witnessed. "Dude...move on."

Joey shrugged. "She wants me. I can wait her out."

"I don't know why you two just don't hook up and get that shit over with," Deena said, shaking her head as she pulled Aris away.

"Where are you taking me?" Aris snapped.

"I have someone I'd like you to meet."

"Deena—"

"You will meet him, and you will like it." She winked at Aris. "Come on...you've been solo since you got here. That shit ain't normal so look at this as me doing you a favor...you're welcome."

After Deena dragged Aris to the other end of the bar, they came to an abrupt stop in front of a guy who had been lingering near the group but seemed to be more comfortable sitting alone at a table. He had a beer in his hand that he casually lifted to his mouth as he stood to greet them, his eyes locked on Aris.

"Meet Jacob." Deena grinned, obviously pleased with her attempt at matchmaking. "Jacob, this is—"

"Aris," he said, his eyes never leaving her face. "I recognize you from the show...you should have won."

"Thank you...Jacob." She looked at Deena, who was already slinking away to give them privacy. Turning to face Jacob, she smiled awkwardly before easing into the chair next to him. "Nice of you to say."

"Are you glad it's over?"

She looked at him curiously. "Why would I be glad?"

"Just a hunch. You don't really strike me as the type who likes to be in front of the camera."

"I do what I have to do." She observed him. "Are you a friend of Deena's?"

"Not really. We had a class together."

"You're a CMDI student?"

"Former student," he replied with a grin. "I finished up about a year ago, but I come back occasionally to use the lab. That's where I was when Deena came through and invited everybody to your celebration. Sorry I didn't make the viewing party, but I'm pretty sure you didn't miss me."

She laughed. "I didn't know half the people in our apartment, and I know even less in here. This is more of a party for Deena than it is for me." She grinned at him. "To add to your surprisingly astute assessment, I'm not big on being the center of attention either."

Another grin. "Something else we have in common."

Finally at ease, Aris leaned back in her chair as they fell into an easy conversation about her work and the intricacies of the show. For a moment, she felt herself bragging about making it into the Top 5 before getting eliminated. Given that sixteen other contestants got the axe before her, she continued to gush. After thirteen long, grueling weeks, she had every damn right to feel proud of herself right now, and she refused to minimize her accomplishment.

Attractive and quite charming, Jacob was the kind of

guy that she could easily spend the rest of the night getting to know in the same way she had come to know David, Shane and Ralph...only this time, it just felt like she shouldn't. Soon, she found herself feeling anxious...but not in a good way.

Because of Luke.

The feeling was so absurd that she looked away from Jacob and stared at the floor, searching herself for the truth...and when what that truly meant dawned on her, she placed a hand over her mouth to cover her amusement, doing her best not to start laughing at herself and the hopelessness of the situation. It had been weeks since she'd spoken to him, since she'd left him sitting on that bench after their argument outside of the restaurant in Santa Monica and here she was, talking to an available and attractive guy, and instead of trying to move on with him, *as she should*, all she could think about was Luke.

A few disrespectful giggles slipped from her mouth.

"You all right over there?"

She glanced at Jacob and wiped her eyes, doing her best to hold in her laughter but it spilled out again as she found herself completely unable to play this age-old game with him. In her mind and in her heart, it was pointless. Luke had stolen both, and there just wasn't room for anyone else.

He had officially fucked her up for life.

Placing a hand on Jacob's arm, she held his gaze. "This isn't going to work. I'm sorry." She took a deep breath and admitted the truth—the crazy, euphoric, ridiculous truth—for the first time...out loud. "I'm in love with someone."

Jacob looked down and took a long sip of beer.

"It's complicated," she added for no particularly reason but to fill the sudden silence between them. For a moment, she was slightly embarrassed. They were in the middle of a great conversation and here she goes blurting her feelings for another man. Awkward.

"That is unfortunate, but I appreciate your honesty," he finally replied. "Guess it's really true what they say, huh? Timing's everything." He grinned and touched her hand. "All the best to you, Aris Collier."

"Same to you, Jacob."

As soon as he left the table, Deena appeared swinging her bottle of beer and wearing a satisfied grin. "This is the part where you thank me...go."

"Thank you," Aris said, standing to hug her. "For making me accept that I am completely in love with a man who has ruined me for the rest of my life."

Pulling the beer bottle from her mouth, Deena turned her head as beer spewed from her mouth. "Wait," she said, a look of shock on her face. "What?!"

"Yes, ma'am. I am in love, and his name is Luke Donovan." She looped her arm in Deena's and hauled her back to the bar to join their friends. "I'll tell you all about him later, but right now...I need booze. Lots and lots of booze."

~ 30 ~

APRIL

Luke opened his refrigerator and stared at the mostly empty shelves. Luckily, there was one beer left from his last grocery run a few weeks ago, so he pulled it out and carried it back to the sofa. After weeks on the road, it felt good to be in his apartment and he looked forward to finally sleeping in his own bed tonight.

Just as quickly as he was feeling gratitude for being home for a while, Devin called and let him know that they'd be back on the road in less than forty-eight hours for a three-week stint. The two of them just stepped off a plane a few hours ago and planned to spend the last two weeks of April in Dallas before getting on the road the first of May, but Devin received a message on his way home from the airport they'd both been anticipating for months.

"First stop is St. Louis then Chicago, Cleveland,

Philly and Boston."

"Cool," he replied, his voice unable to project the excitement that he actually felt.

"Hey, you good?" Devin asked after a brief pause.

Luke rubbed his eyes and chuckled, knowing what Devin was really asking him. "Yeah. And for the last time...I'm sure. Calling it quits after all these years together is never easy, but it was for the best."

Another pause. "Have you told Aris yet?"

"Why?"

"Why not? After all, you did it for her...right?"

Luke had asked himself that same question more times than he cared to admit since he'd broken up with Jessica and resigned his position at Knox Corp.

Ending his relationship had been hard. Moving on was proving to be much harder. It would be easy to go back and pick up the pieces, but every time the thought surfaced, he buried it. He'd already tried that, out of guilt, and it had failed...because while he had been focusing on repairing their relationship, Jessica had been more concerned with running Knox Corp in her father's absence.

Over the past few months, Mr. Knox's health had stabilized. When he was released from the hospital, everyone expected him to be walking the halls the following day as was his nature. However, he shocked everyone by announcing that he was in the process of officially transitioning his duties to his daughter.

Jessica could not have been more thrilled.

With such status came a need for more stability and, out of nowhere, Jessica began insisting on an instant engagement and fall wedding. Not that Luke was completely thrown because marriage had always been the plan for them, but they weren't in love anymore. More than that, they were different people now. And given how increasingly disconnected he'd felt and Jessica seemed to be doing it more for optics than ardor gave him the courage to finally do what needed to be done...for both of them.

Initially, Jessica had dissolved into tears followed by the worst fight of their entire relationship. But once the dust settled, something miraculous happened. They parted with mutual respect and genuine wishes for the very best for each other. And given how much he truly cared for her, it was a relief to Luke to know that they hadn't lost everything between them.

The next week, they began in-depth discussions regarding the "dissolution" of their relationship. Jessica's terminology, ever the strategist. Luke let her know that he'd do whatever was necessary to spin it in a positive light and maintain everyone's focus on her ability to assume her rightful role and take the helm of her father's company.

With the weight of their failing relationship off the table, Luke was able to really *see* Jessica for the first time in months...and it saddened him. No one really understood how much pressure she always put on herself. Not the way he did.

In addition to her anxiety about her father's health, Jessica was becoming uncharacteristically insecure right before his eyes. It was a lot for her and Luke knew she desperately needed to give herself a break, but he also knew she had something to prove, to him and to everyone else, so he did the only thing he could do...he gave her the space and unconditional support she needed to spread her wings and *be* Jessica Knox — without guilt, pressure or judgment.

Luke dutifully did his part by ensuring that she ate often and slept regularly, two things she always let slip. He also did his best to attend as many parties, happy hours, meetings and events that she could cram onto their schedules — not as her man but as the guy who had always believed in her...because he still did and always would.

Though he was focused on her success, his energy and drive doubled for himself. It was time for him to believe in himself. To step out from the shadow of the Knox name and build the company he always wanted. To be his own man.

"Nah, man," Luke said, finally answering Devin's question. "I did it for me."

"I hear you."

"What time's the flight again?"

"Leaves at seven-forty," Devin replied. "You already sound like shit and this next leg is gonna be brutal, so get some rest."

"I'm good."

"Yeah. One."

Ending the call, Luke grabbed the remote and pressed a button to select his recent DVR recordings. When he found what he was looking for, he pressed play and settled back against the sofa with his food in his lap. Never in a million years would he have ever watched this show, but thanks to Aris, he was tuned in like it was the NFL playoffs.

He'd found out about it a few weeks ago when he

ran into Kim at the mall. He was shopping for a birthday gift to ship to his mother when he heard someone call his name. He'd been surprised when he turned to see Kim, looking well and back on her feet.

He'd asked her about her recovery, careful not to mention Aris too often during their conversation, but Kim had given him a knowing look. It was obvious that she was aware of what happened between him and Aris in Los Angeles. She had probably gotten an earful the minute Aris picked her up from the airport later that evening...but, despite what she knew, Kim still answered every question about Aris that he hadn't had the nerve to ask.

Maybe she'd felt sorry for him.

He couldn't hide how much he was missing her.

After leaving the mall, he'd driven home deep in thought. The minute he entered his apartment, he grabbed the remote to search for that *FleshFX* show that Kim had told him about. Once he found it, he programmed his DVR to record all the upcoming episodes. Then, he relaxed on the sofa to watch the first episode On Demand. The moment he saw Aris on screen that first time, striking a pose during the opening credits, he'd smiled with pride.

The same way he was doing right now.

Luke sat up and placed his elbows on his knees. After an internal debate, he grabbed his phone and stared at it. Then, he unlocked it tapped out a short text message...the first communication between them since their fight in the parking lot.

Congratulations on the show. You didn't suck today.

He pressed SEND.

Tossing the phone to the other end of the sofa, he leaned back against the cushions and played another episode he'd missed while traveling.

He wondered how she was really doing.

If she was happy.

His phone buzzed.

Turning his head, he glanced at the phone. He had no reason to believe she would want to hear from him, never mind respond to his message. But he hoped like hell it was her. Grabbing his phone again, he shook his head at the anxiety he felt as he pressed the envelope icon on home screen.

Thanks. Bet you did though.

He grinned, tapping out a reply.

Guilty. I'm totally useless to the universe.

He waited. A moment later, his phone buzzed again.

Not to me.

Her response surprised him.

He stared at the screen, debating on how he should respond. Just as he was about to tell her he missed her, another message appeared.

I need your help with something.

With what?

I need you to be my star. Wanna come out west?

He laughed at the absurdity of her question, at the absurdity of even *asking* him that question and expecting any reply other than "hell yeah."

Just say when.

After a few more exchanges, they stopped texting, so she could get back to work. Placing his phone on the cushion next to him, he returned his attention to her smiling face as her on-screen persona exclaimed how excited she was about her idea for the Week's Challenge during her confessional.

Luke relaxed and kept his eyes on her...

And by the end of the night, he was completely caught up.

~ *31* ~

JULY

Approaching baggage claim, Luke spotted Aris standing near the carousel donning a chauffeur's hat and holding a cardboard sign in her hands with colorful, cartoonish letters that read, *Comic-Con Model*.

"You're an artist," he said as he stopped in front of her. "But you can't make a decent sign?"

"Whatever." She rose to her toes and gave him a big hug. "It's a great sign. And good morning to you, too. Welcome to San Diego!"

Realizing that there were no checked bags to wait for, she led him out to the parking deck. Once they were inside her car, she chucked her hat, turned to him and smiled. "Are you hungry?"

"Are you going to finally give me the details about what exactly you need me to do this weekend?"

"Sheesh...always in such a rush," she replied,

wrinkling her nose. "Can't ask how I'm doing or how my morning is going...nooo...you gotta get—"

"Stop stalling."

"Okay, okay. I...need...you...to..."

He glared at her and she laughed.

"Okay, for real...I need you to be my partner for the Masquerade at Comic-Con in San Diego." She squealed and clapped her hands before settling them back on the steering wheel. "Cool, right?!"

"So that's the big reveal? You need me to take you to a party?" He reclined his seat, unfazed. "Cool."

"Kinda sorta...it's more like an onstage costume competition."

He turned his head to look at her. "A talent show?"

"Basically, yeah. And I want you to be in it...with me. We're gonna be a duo!"

He frowned. "A what?"

"It took a while for me to come up with a concept but I finally settled on an eighties fantasy schtick theme." She held up hands up like she was literally framing her idea. "*Labyrinth* meets *The Neverending Story*."

"I vaguely remember seeing those movies as a kid," he replied. "Didn't one of them have terrible life lessons or something?"

"Ugh, stop being so judgy," she said as she started the engine. "Anyway, I was thinking we could play two temperamental friends with personality issues. Your creature will be a mix of two characters from each movie, and I'll be a mix of two others. I've got a skit and the whole nine...just a few lines, nothing major. You're gonna love it..."

"Great," he replied, his voice less than enthused.

She turned to stare at him. "Please, please don't bail."

Noticing the fear in her eyes, Luke grinned and patted her leg in reassurance. "Calm down. I got you."

"You mean it? You'll really do it?"

"Yes, I mean it and I'll really do it. Whatever you got planned, I'm all yours this weekend."

Apparently thrilled with his response, she began yammering on and on about colors, fabrics, makeup and materials. He was able to keep up with most of it until she began giving him back story on his characters. By the time they made it to her apartment, he still had no idea what the hell *The Nothing* really was, but he pretended that he had full understanding so she wouldn't have to explain it to him a third time.

Luke was surprised when Aris checked them into a two-room suite at the convention center hotel. It was her gift of comfort to him for being such a good sport about being her model. He tried to convince her to downgrade considering that they would barely be in the suite with all the activities going on during the weekend, but she would hear nothing of it. She simply grinned after telling him to shut up and enjoy it for the time they would be in it.

Their afternoon was spent lounging around in their hotel suite until her roommate, Deena, and the rest of their CMDI crew arrived and joined them. Amazingly, Luke was able to keep up with their nerd convo pretty well given his new knowledge of special effects thanks to his many hours of watching *FleshFX*.

When the sun went down, they left the hotel and headed to a party at Joey's cousin's girlfriend's house on the other side of town. The price of admission was liquor, and they each had a bottle in hand as they were welcomed into the house. After the first fifteen minutes, Aris and Luke broke away from the crew and ventured into the backyard where they found a sea of people enjoying themselves as music filled the air.

"What are you doing?" Luke asked as he watched Aris wiggling around in her usual awkward fashion.

Laughing, she eased her body closer to his. "Come on, gorgeous...it's a party. Get into it." Pulling him out into the middle of the crowd, she danced with him until she was breathless. Smiling ear to ear, she two-stepped toward him until she was directly in his face. "Are you having fun yet, Luke Donovan?"

Grabbing her waist, he pulled her against him and slowed their pace. In the midst of all the bouncing bodies, they began to rock slowly, the fingers of his right hand doing dangerous things to her lower back. "Absolutely."

Shifting away from his touch, Aris pulled Luke out of the crowd toward an empty table. As they sat, she felt his eyes on her but she continued people-watching, trying to control her breathing. She noticed him slip away and return moments later with a beer in each hand. Grateful, she snatched one and took a long swig to quench her thirst.

"Easy," he said, laughing. "I should've brought you some water."

"No, you did right." She took another sip, her eyes

catching his as she pulled the bottle from her lips and sat it on the table. "I'm glad you're here."

"I'm glad you needed me."

In her mind, she was beginning to believe that she would always need him but she didn't allow the words to escape her mouth. Instead, she took another sip and grinned. "Thanks again though. I know it wasn't easy breaking away from your monster schedule.

"You ask, I come," he replied, a sexy smile on his face as his eyes swept her face. "I'm easy like that."

"What?!" She laughed. Long and hard. Impressed that he so easily quoted one of her favorite television shows. "Now you watch teen vamp soaps? Man...I think I'm getting under your skin."

His gaze never wavered. "In the best way."

Her eyes dropped to his lips as her body responded, desire flooding her core. "We should probably go," she blurted, forcing herself to look away and search the crowd for her friends.

Luke followed her back into the house, and she found Deena right outside of the kitchen making drinks. When she told her that they were turning in for the night, Deena winked conspiratorially before giving her a hug.

Turning to Luke, Deena smiled. "Take care of my girl...we'll see you tomorrow at Comic-Con."

"Always," he replied easily. "Be safe getting back to the hotel."

Minutes later, Luke and Aris were walking to her car. Directing her to the passenger side, Luke opened her door and helped her inside. The ride was quiet. When they finally entered the hotel suite, Luke stared at her until she began to wring her hands. He turned away, blowing out a heavy breath. "Shit...I just can't help it. I'm sor—"

"Don't apologize."

And then, without thinking, she closed the distance between them and placed her hands on his back before moving them up to his shoulders, encouraging him to turn and face her. She bit her lip as she gazed at his mouth and then lifted her eyes to meet his. "I get it. I love you too."

He visibly relaxed as he stared at her, the hint of a smile playing at his lips as he brushed his hand across her cheek, caressing her face. "Moody, I—"

She gently pressed a finger against his lips. "But it doesn't mean that we're supposed to be together."

They stood quietly, facing each other until he finally spread his arms and she stepped into his embrace, hugging him as he placed a gentle kiss on her forehead.

"Goodnight, Luke Donovan."

Pulling away from his warmth, she turned and walked into her room.

Alone.

~ 32 ~

Aris propped herself up in bed, deciding to give up her attempts at slumber and accept that sleep wasn't going to happen for her tonight. She grabbed her cell phone from the nightstand but put it back where it was a minute later. Sinking back under the sheets, she stared into the darkness and grumbled.

She was so tired of failing.

Though coming in fourth place on the show was pretty impressive by anyone's standards, she'd still been disappointed...but also secretly relieved at the same time. She didn't know what she had been thinking trying to balance school, her internship and taping the show at the same time. So many days, she had been on the verge of burnout but she kept pushing, kept her mind focused on her work...so she wouldn't have to think about the man she was currently sharing a hotel suite with...

The way she was thinking of him now.

Since her eyes opened two hours ago and stayed that way, she'd been pretending that her restlessness had everything to do with her desire to win the Best Original Design category later on that night. It was better for her to believe that was the source of her insomnia, to restrain herself with more productive thoughts, to concern herself with things that were within her reach, with things she could actually have.

Flinging the covers off, she forced herself from the bed and began toying around with her mannequins until the sun came up. When she heard Luke stirring an hour later, she allowed herself to stroll into the living room that connected their separate bedrooms and finally face him.

Surprisingly, he was already showered and dressed, the scent of his cologne teasing her. He was stretched out on the sofa, watching television. His eyes looked a bit tired, as if he had also lost his bout with sleep.

It was silly, really. How hard they were both fighting what could be so easy between them, but it was the right thing to do...even if they did both feel and look like complete shit today because of it.

He glanced at her. "Hey."

She lifted her hand to wave at him like a dork but quickly redirected it to her hair. "Hey."

"I can go grab breakfast for us if you're hungry."

"No. Thanks. Not enough time. I have a few check-in things to do for the Masquerade in about an hour. I'll just grab a muffin or some fruit or something from the café in the lobby."

He nodded. "You need some help taking all that stuff

down there?"

"Yeah. Thanks." She ran a hand over her hair and sighed. "So...I'll just go get dressed now."

Slipping back into her room, she began her routine. Checking off her mental list of items in the shower. Double-checking her cases of materials as she drip-dried and brushed her teeth. An hour later, she emerged from her bedroom and found a sleeping Luke stretched out and snoring on the sofa.

"Don't make me leave you."

He jerked his head at her voice and sat up slowly. "Just fell off for a minute. I'm ready."

She grabbed his hand and pulled him to his feet. Smiling up at him, she was about to tell him that she would loan him her shoulder to sleep on when they boarded the plane, but the words caught in her throat when she locked eyes with him. Suddenly, she became keenly aware of how close they were. It was insane how quickly and easily he could shift her from cool to crazed as he was doing now, generating a pressure within her that cut a narrow path straight to her core the same way it had the night before...and every other time they were alone together.

"Aris."

She blinked. "Huh?"

He grinned. "You're gonna be late."

"Yeah." She gripped the handle of the smallest rolling case while he handled the rest. "Let's go."

The journey down to the main lobby was equally, the confines of the elevator laced with tension and filled with everything they refused to say to each other. Restless, she kept her eyes trained on the numbers above the doors, counting down the floors, bouncing her leg until Luke's hand covered hers and she relaxed.

The moment they stepped through the main entrance of the convention center, it was nonstop madness and pleasurable chaos. Fortunately, Luke was the perfect calm to her storm as she raced about to recreate the visions in her mind for tonight's Masquerade. Deena and Zach arrived shortly after they did, ready to get to work. Luke decided to stick around while the three of them completed the major costume and design details, amazed at their collective talents.

By late afternoon, it was time for Luke and Aris to get weighed down with materials and makeup. Luke's transformation into a Fox-Terrier-Werewolf was spectacular, a stark contrast to the delicate beauty of Aris as a Firey-Sphinx. Practicing their lines, they joked around and also ad-libbed a bit, their natural chemistry enhancing the script as they went along.

In the end, Aris's vision turned out to be the perfect blend of the two epic fantasies, both of their characters a complement to the other in color and concept...and the crowd loved it.

Aris strutted onto the stage, her wings on magnificent display as she sang a quirky, soulful remix about letting the good times roll. She bumped into Luke who exaggerated his role as a brave and honorable knight as he broke her fall. At first, Luke maintained his character's stiff demeanor but as Aris pressured him into joining her in some wild adventures, he loosened up and caved to her charms. As soon as he did, Aris flipped her personality, physically extending the intricately painted, scaly wings on her back as she judged him harshly for not being the purposeful knight he claimed to be. Angered by Aris's harsh criticism and shedding his honorable façade, Luke removed his massive helmet and oversized costume to reveal his true werewolf personality and costuming, a masterful blend of wild hair and makeup over a sculptured, prosthetic physique, complete with cracked vertebrae, hand spikes and an exquisitely gruesome, hardened canine face. Flashing his fangs, Luke chased Aris around the stage and tried to rip her to shreds until she switched back to her Firey side and laughed hysterically, telling him to lighten up and that she was only teasing. Hopping onto his back, she guaranteed that a juicy burger would taste much better than she did and she knew just the place to get it. Donning his helmet once again, Luke chivalrously carried Aris on his back on their way to the diner, teasing each other as they exited stage left.

Hearing the thunderous applause backstage, Aris squealed and threw her arms around Luke in celebration. "That was so much fun...and oh my God, do you hear that?! They loved it!"

Before he could respond, they were surrounded by Deena and Zach as well as other contestants who showered them with compliments and cheers. When the applause quieted, Luke and Aris returned to the side of the stage to enjoy the remaining performances.

Feeling how nervous she was, Luke held her hand and didn't let go until they announced the winners for each category. When Best Original Design was called, she closed her eyes and tried to steady her breathing.

"In third place...*Freaks of Nature* with design by Chris Long and Gigi Dodson...make-up by Donna Coles and Howard Jones!

"In second place...*Labyrinth Meets The Neverending Story* with both design and make-up by Aris Collier!

Though her heart dropped at the loss of first place, Aris squeezed Luke's hand and eagerly pulled him into the spotlight with her, each step toward her trophy validating her talent, finally shifting her to a genuine place of both appreciation and pride for being respected among her peers.

Aris and Luke continued to stand side-by-side as the winners were called—a team of artists from Reno whose *Creepy Circus Clique* won over the judges.

Turning away from Aris, Luke stooped down low enough for her to hop onto his shoulders and he paraded her around and off the stage to a resounding chorus of cheers before they followed Deena and the CMDI crew out of the ballroom.

After the ceremony ended and the crowd dispersed, Luke smiled as Aris continued celebrating with her crew. He knew in her heart that she wanted first place, but he was glad that she recognized just how amazing it was for her to be crowned a Top 3 Artist.

"Let's go out!" Deena said, excitedly. "This level of awesomeness requires a real and foolish celebration... who's in?"

Without pause, everyone screamed, "IN!"

Aris laughed and turned to Luke. "Coming?"

"Wouldn't miss it."

Her eyes sparkled as she looked up at him. "Whaaat? Mr. I-Need-To-Know-Everything is not even going to ask where we're going?"

He grinned and kissed her forehead. "As long as you're there, it doesn't matter."

After leaving the convention center, they all piled in cars and cruised to a run-down strip that owned a neighborhood dive that time forgot, but apparently no one got the memo because there were cars lined up and down both sides of the street. After circling the block, they found a paved parking area and got ripped off but at least they had a better chance of their cars still being there when they were ready to leave. Danny teased Joey about his incredible ability to always find the absolute worst places in every city across the country but, given that Joey's family was from San Diego, we decided to trust him this time. Flipping us all off, Joey bet Danny twenty bucks that they were all about to have the time of their lives.

And he won.

Though its exterior seemed pretty bland, the interior of the pub was crawling with people of all shapes, sizes and colors. There was a *Cheers*-sized bar along with pool tables, a sound stage, a live band and dozens of flat screens because sports always works for crowds.

They immediately crashed the bar and did a few shots before they ventured near the stage to take part in an amateur singing competition that even the most snobbish karaoke rats could get into.

Danny led the way, easing through the tight crowd

until he found a wall to hug on the left side of the stage. Luke moved toward the narrow space next to him and leaned his back against it, pulling Aris so she could relax against him.

"Did you explain the rules?" Deena yelled at Aris, nodding her head in Luke's direction.

Aris turned her head and curved her finger for him. He ducked his head, his ear near her lips. "Everybody sings at least once. That's the rule."

"Oh, in that case…hell no."

Aris laughed, having already expected his response. She already knew that getting Luke on stage would take no less than an act of God, but she and her friends still tried to hype him up to do it anyway.

Danny went first with an old school hip hop song and then Joey and Zach did a sloppy rendition of a popular country hit that had the crowd in stitches. Deena went up next, pulling Danny in for their own duo which was so raunchy that the crowd yelled for an encore. By that time, Luke and Aris had confiscated a few abandoned tables and pulled them together and Leslie had ordered another two rounds of drinks. When Deena made it back to the table, she took another shot of liquor and slammed it on the table.

"You ready, chica?" she slurred, her eyes on Aris.

Aris glanced at Luke and smiled. "If you'll excuse me…I gotta show these amateurs how it's really done."

Luke laughed as she whispered something in Deena's ear before sashaying to the stage. Deena grinned and grabbed Leslie, rushing to catch up with her. She chatted briefly with the DJ and he nodded, quickly getting things ready for their performance.

With Deena and Leslie on her left and right, Aris grabbed the microphone and the men went wild and started whistling and cat-calling. "Hol' up, hol' up... before y'all get too excited, let me manage y'alls expectations. I know we fine as hell, but this ain't about to be no Destiny's Child type shit." She blew a kiss to a guy standing at the front of the stage who dramatically grabbed his chest like he was heartbroken. She winked at him. "Sorry, boo."

When the laughter died down, Aris looked up into the strobe light and then gazed out into the audience. "I *am* feeling good tonight though...'cause you see, I just left Comic-Con...yes, yes, thank you...and you know what? I did something I never really believed I could do...but I did that shit tonight. And you know what else? I won second-place...which is a pretty big fucking deal if I do say so myself!"

The crowd roared.

"So tonight, I'm gonna do a little something to honor this good feeling I have going on and to remind all of you that the sky's the limit." She smiled brightly as the music and background vocals of the track began. "This one's for Luke, who's looking at me right now like I'm crazy...nah, I just figured since I'm living my dreams right now, I may as well handle my rock star fantasies too...let's go!"

Shaking his head, Luke watched as she closed her eyes and began singing the first few verses. His eyes shifted as he noticed the shift in the crowd, a wave of shock silencing them when they realized that Aris could really sing. Deena and Leslie brought the sexy in the background, patiently waiting until Aris's vocals swelled along with the piano chords and marching percussion and then they finally joined in, rocking out to the chorus and bouncing around the stage like it was a real concert. Then, Aris stepped back up to the microphone stand for the dramatic monologue, hyping the crowd up even more as she spoke out being different, ignoring the naysayers, overcoming your adversities and living your dreams.

It was magical.

Bobbing his head, all Luke could do was smile.

When the song was over, everyone was on their feet screaming for more. Aris, Deena and Leslie wrapped their arms around each other and thanked the audience before snaking their way back to their tables, accepting compliments and high-fives all along the way. When Aris reached Luke, she flashed a brilliant smile and threw her arms around his neck.

"Take notes," she said, pulling away to catch his eyes before she winked. "That's what two-minute *slayage* looks like...no autographs, please."

He reached up and swept the hair away from her face. The urge to kiss her was so profound that he was grinding his teeth.

But it wasn't right.

At least not right at that moment.

Instead, he kissed her forehead and bumped the small fist she held up for him. As soon as they touched, they opened their hands to mimic an explosion, adding sound effects and all before they laughed.

After another hour of foolishness, the crew filed out of the building and into the cool, night air. When Deena asked if they were tagging along to the next spot, Aris grabbed Luke's hand to signal her plans for the rest of the night.

Several hugs and goodbyes later, Luke and Aris hopped into their rental car in search of a late night snack. They found a diner ten miles away with as many people inside as the bar they'd just left. Once they settled into their booth, they placed their orders and fell into an easy chat. She carried most of the conversation because he was too busy staring at her.

In the middle of another story she was telling him about her and Deena, she looked in his eyes and paused. When he didn't respond right away, she began to blush. "What?"

"I love you, Aris Collier."

She bit her lip and gave him an easy smile. "I love you too, Luke Donovan."

"It's cold over here. You should come sit with me."

Before the last word left his mouth, she slipped out of the booth and joined him on his side. Grabbing a piece of fresh bread that the server dropped at their table, he split it and handed a piece to her. She put it in her mouth right away.

"Why didn't you ever pursue it?"

"Pursue what?" she asked, still chewing.

"Singing."

She glanced at him and shrugged. "My Dad. When I was in elementary school and he realized I had a voice, he sort of freaked out about it. Reminded him too much of my Mom, I guess."

"Tell me about her."

Unsure of what her response to his question would be, Luke was relieved when she smiled. "She was a local jazz singer. As the story goes, my Dad saw her in a club once and he kept going back, night after night until she agreed to go out with him. They fell in love pretty fast after that. When she started to blow up and get more gigs, he dropped out of school to follow her overseas...and then I popped up." She glanced at him, her smile fading. "I remember singing a song for him on his birthday. I was seven, and I didn't understand at the time why it made him cry. I thought it was because he was proud of me, but...well, let's just say I didn't want to make him cry again so I stopped singing after that. Sure, it was something I could do but, just because you can do something doesn't always mean you should."

He grabbed her hand under the table, threading his fingers through hers.

"Besides, makeup was my true passion. Just the thought of being able to explore colors and designs was everything to me. It was the only thing that really made me feel complete. Like I'd found what I was meant to do." She gave him the side eye. "I could ask you the same question, you know."

When he raised an eyebrow, she twisted her mouth and nudged him with her shoulder.

"I know how much you want to run away from bureaucracy," she explained. "Why didn't you?"

It was his turn to shrug. "I guess when you do something for so long, it just becomes easier. In college, I didn't have a real idea of who I was. I just knew I wanted to be successful. So when life presented my best option, I was all over it. At the time, it looked and seemed right, but then again I was measuring success the way others viewed it. People had all these expectations for me, and I just didn't want to let them down, y'know? But after a while, I started to feel restless. Like there had to be more to life than what I was doing. It's like I woke up one day and drew a blank. I had no idea how I'd gotten to where I was or why I was even doing what I was doing and trying to force it to feel right...and I wasn't sure how to find my way back."

"To what?"

"Peace." He shook his head. "But it didn't make sense for me to stop. I'd made it this far. I figured it was just a phase and I'd get through it. But there comes a moment when you realize that you're running really fast in the wrong direction...and that's when you turn around, find your way and hope for the best."

"And now?"

He smiled at her. "I'm almost there."

Under the table, she squeezed his hand.

"I have you to thank for that."

"Me?"

"When I met you, you were so sure about who you are. Even now, it's been difficult for you but you never lose sight of...you. Despite what others think or expect, what looks good or makes the most sense, what you should do or what's most appropriate...you stay true to who Aris is, and you win or lose on your own merit. You are unapologetically, authentically you...all over the place. You have no idea how much I respect that, how impressive that is. I appreciate you, Aris Collier."

"Thank you," she replied, her eyes wide. "I'm... wow. That means a lot coming from you."

"I meant every word. You're the shit, girl...and I'm going to be like you when I grow up."

That made her laugh. "Like me, huh? A struggling artist sitting on a profitable, technical degree but working minimum wage, living check-to-check and chasing a pipe dream while basically existing on a wing and a prayer?"

He stared at her, affection in his eyes. "Like a person who lives on purpose."

"Damn...I'm all that, huh?"

"All that and more."

Smiling from ear to ear, she squeezed his hand again. "I've really missed you. There's been so much I've wanted to tell you over these last few months but..."

"But what?"

"It was wrong for me to keep popping in and out of your life that way...especially when I knew how I really felt about you. And now that you're engaged —"

"Wait, what?" he asked, searching her eyes. "We never got engaged...where did you get that from?"

"Oh," she replied, looking down. "I saw an article online...Kim's squad won a championship, and I was looking for it and found...anyway. Never mind that." She shrugged again and forced another smile. "How are you and Jessica anyway? I'm sure she's just as excited that you're finding your way back to being yourself again." She glanced at him, curiously. "So when exactly do you plan to pop the question?"

"We'll talk about all that some other time," he said just before the server interrupted to place their entrees on the table. Perfect timing. "I'm more interested in all this stuff you've kept from me."

As they ate, he listened intently as Aris told him about everything he'd missed, about everything she'd done for herself since he'd last seen her in L.A. What stood out most was how much more focused she was now, how much this time on her own had meant to her. How much she'd grown and how much she was enjoying the feeling of having no one to please but Aris. It appeared—at least to him—that for the first time in her adult life, she was loving and taking care of herself.

Which was why he decided to hold off on telling her about his breakup with Jessica and expressing his desire for Aris to be more than his friend. He didn't want to pressure her or to derail her dreams. Now was the time for her to decide what she really wanted out of life, and he didn't want to get in the way of that.

He had to let her go…at least for now.

He loved her enough to wait until she was ready.

~ 33 ~

Aris woke up in a great mood and decided to order room service and surprise Luke with breakfast in bed, but she realized the flaw in her plan the minute she entered his room and saw his back exposed, the sheet dangerously low on his hips.

Was he completely naked under there?

Shaking off her body's response to the thought, she kicked the door with her foot. "Wake up, sleepyhead!"

He groaned in response and peeked his head from underneath a pillow. "C'mon, Moody...I already know you're not a morning person, so what is this about?" He blinked and emerged further from underneath the pillow and grinned when he saw the tray in her hands.

What happened next was enough to make her and the food drop to the floor but she caught herself. Tossing off the covers, Luke stood in nothing more than boxers and stretched. "Give me a minute...you can climb in and get started if you want."

"Uhh…this is just for you. M-mine is in my room."

"Then go get it and meet me back here," he said casually, walking into the bathroom.

It wasn't a request.

After he closed the door, she closed her eyes and tried to force her waves to calm but it was no use. She shook her head in amazement. There was never a moment when she didn't want this man and, given her sexual history, that in itself was remarkable.

"What are you doing to me?" she mumbled to herself, both pleased and terrified by the affect he had on her. Placing the tray on the end of the bed, she left his room and took a little longer than necessary to retrieve her own tray of food as she debated whether or not she could really handle her big, bright idea of breakfast in bed *with* Luke.

"Moody…where you at?"

"Coming!"

Grabbing her tray of food, she stopped by the kitchenette to grab a few extra paper towels before heading to his room. When she entered, he had on a tee and basketball shorts and, though she felt relieved, she was already missing the naked version of him.

Fortunately, she survived breakfast, choosing to talk incessantly about their plans for the day. They shared each other's food and when it was all eaten, they curled up and watched a pay-per-view movie. Well, he watched it. She just tried to lie there as normally as possible but, in the end, she managed to survive the movie too.

After getting dressed, they checked out, stored their

luggage in the car and returned to the convention center. This time, the pressure of the competition was off so they were able to fully explore the exhibits, catch a few indie films, view original works at the art show and sign up for a two-on-two Pokemon tournament.

Walking back to the car at the end of a very full day, arm-in-arm, Aris looked up at Luke and smiled. "Thanks for humoring me."

"No problem...I actually had a great time. I've always heard of Comic-Con but never knew what it was really about." He tweaked her nose. "Now I do."

"And you can tell everyone that you're now the first-place Pokemon champion."

"Yeah, uhh...no."

An hour later, they arrived at the airport. Aris parked her car and followed Luke inside. He decided to check his bag at the last minute, so she sat on a nearby bench and waited until he was done. When he returned to her, she stood up and smiled.

"You made my weekend, Luke Donovan."

"Sorry it has to end," he replied. He stepped closer and kissed her forehead. "But I'm glad it happened."

"Me too."

They hugged each other a little too long, and Aris was the first to pull away. They smiled at each other before turning in opposite directions — Aris walking back to her car to start her drive back to L.A. while Luke headed toward airport security to catch his flight back to Dallas.

~ 34 ~

SEPTEMBER

Late nights. Early mornings.

Caffeine. Caffeine. Caffeine.

The weeks after Comic-Con had been a whirlwind as Aris worked to complete her program. Her final class was her favorite but also the most difficult one to complete, which made it even more rewarding when she aced it.

It was amazing how quickly the months went by, even more so how much she'd accomplished in such a short time. Not only was she now an official graduate of one of the top makeup schools in the country and a second-place Masquerade winner at Comic-Con, but she was also financially stable for the first time in a long while. Not to mention her stint on *FleshFX* was still generating quite a bit of buzz despite her being eliminated and not making it to the finale.

The day she received her diploma was the proudest day of her life, and she celebrated her achievements the entire weekend with a tub of frozen yogurt and a *Walking Dead* DVD marathon.

But when Monday morning reared its ugly head, Aris couldn't help but contemplate her next move. Los Angeles had been good to her, but she had no idea if she could afford to live there permanently. Now that her program was complete and her internship was over, she had to capitalize on them and fast. Getting a job at the mall or in a boutique like before was an immediate fix, but she rejected that option before it could fully form in her mind.

No going back. Only forward. Always forward.

If she was going to be serious about her new career, she had to find credible, relevant work now.

But first, she had some packing to do.

Aris was finishing up her laundry and organizing her mannequins when Deena strolled through the front door, bags in hand, fresh from a shopping trip.

"You know we don't have to be out of here for another two weeks right?" Deena said, shutting the door behind her. "What's the rush?"

"No rush. Getting it out of the way, that's all."

"Well, the slacker in me will be waiting until the eleventh hour…unless I get a call to jet to work on location somewhere, preferably tropical."

Aris laughed. "From your mouth to God's ears."

Deena opened her shopping bags to show Aris the results of her afternoon at the mall, and they spent the next twenty minutes debating the best outfit for a blind date Deena had later that evening. Once a decision was made, Deena helped fold the rest of Aris's laundry.

"Have you given any more thought to where you're going to end up?" Deena asked as they carried baskets of clothing down the hall and entered Aris's bedroom.

Aris shrugged. "Your guess is as good as mine."

"Bullshit, honey," Deena replied, shaking her head as she sat her basket next to Aris's bed. "I will never understand why you just won't go back to Dallas...and when I say Dallas, I mean Luke."

"We're just friends," Aris replied in a sing-song voice to mask her exhaustion for having to explain this to Deena again for the hundredth time.

"Yeah, yeah, yeah...and he's engaged to Black Barbie and all that. I got it." Deena gave Aris a measured glance. "What I don't get is how you can keep playing this game with him when the world can see that you're both in love with each other."

Aris stretched out on her bed. "Dee...don't."

"I'm just saying," Deena replied, holding up her hands in surrender as she headed toward the door. "I love you girl, but you really need to get a clue before you lose what's yours."

"Mine?" Aris rolled her eyes. "For the last time, Luke and Jessica are *to-ge-ther*. Which means Luke and I should *not* be despite what the world sees. Besides, he already has a perfect life with a bright future all laid out for him...who am I to change that?"

Deena released another sigh, shaking her head again as she left the room. "Who are you, indeed?"

Aris opened her eyes and yawned.

Her intent had been to just relax for fifteen minutes after Deena left her bedroom to get ready for her blind date. That was three hours ago and now Deena was gone and she had the apartment to herself.

Rolling over and grabbing the phone from her nightstand, she decided to call Kim.

"Hello?"

"Hey…it's me."

"Hey, girl. Your timing is perfect. Hold on a sec."

Kim clicked over to her other line, and Aris picked at her nails while she waited. Just as she considered scheduling a mani/pedi, Kim came back on the line. "Sorry…you still there?"

"Yep. Now tell me why my timing is so perfect."

"Well, first off missy, I wanted to tell you again how very proud I am of you. I showed everybody at the boutique your graduation picture. I'm still pissed you didn't send me an invitation. Heifa."

"I didn't send anybody an invitation because it wasn't that serious," Aris replied. "You saw the video I sent…the ceremony barely lasted an hour."

"Anyway," Kim said. "Even though I'm only worth cell phone footage of one of the most important days of your life, I still have a surprise for you."

"I hate surprises."

"This I know, but trust me, you'll love this one." She cleared her throat for dramatic effect. "So I'm dating this new guy…"

"Ooh, shocker…and exactly what does that have to do with me?"

"Just shut up and listen," Kim snapped. "So I met

this guy who knows a guy who works for your favorite TV show."

Sensing where this might be going, Aris sat up and listened intently. "Seriously?"

"Yep...so I told my new guy about you and he told the other guy..."

"Just tell me already!"

"His name is Jake Dunn, and he will be in Dallas next weekend and wants to talk to you in person...and he also said he'll be able to work something out for you."

"Seriously?!" She squealed. "Yes! Oh my God...I need to spruce up my portfolio...does he want to see anything else? Like a resume or something? I can get it to him as soon as — "

"Look at you...all industrious now," Kim replied, a smile in her voice. "But actually, there's no need for all of that. The job is yours. Now, it doesn't pay a whole lot, but I thought you'd just be happy to finally be working on a real live set and living your dream like we always said you...hello? Aris? Aris?"

Aris was twirling around the room. When she picked up the phone, she squealed again.

"You're the bestest ever...I just want to squeeze you right now!"

"You're welcome, honey," Kim replied, laughing. I was happy to do it. You know I believe in you. It's just a matter of time before everyone else sees what I see."

"Thank you, thank you, thank you!" she screamed. "I gotta tell Deena, she's gonna freak! Call you back."

Hanging up, she danced some more. Finally calming down, Aris thought over everything Kim had just told her. When she replayed the part where she had to meet the guy, she paused. A second later, she called Kim back instead of texting Deena the great news.

"Yeeesss?"

She frowned at the sarcasm lacing Kim's sing-song voice when she answered. "What's that about?"

"I knew you were going to call me right back."

"Then you know I must be confused about the part where you said the guy wants to talk to me in person."

"And," Kim replied. "What's the problem?"

"Well, if the job is already mine then what's there to talk about?"

"Really, Aris?" Kim asked in a disappointed Mom kind of way.

"Of course, I'll be professional and send an official thank you letter and all that. But that's a hell of a long way for both of us to fly for chit-chat."

"Ugh...Aris he wants to *spend time* with you. As in we're going to double-date, and I need your ass here the weekend after next to make it work."

Aris frowned again. "You really should have led with that."

"Why? So you could be you and say no before I could tell you the whole thing?"

"Kim, if me hooking up with this guy is the prerequisite to getting this job..."

"Eww...no, hell no. I'd never rope you into something like that. You're my girl. I always got you."

"Then clear it up for me."

"Well, he's kind of a fan of yours."

She blinked. "A what?"

"He said he saw you on *FleshFX* and thinks you're uber talented but, above all else, he thinks you're hot.

He also told Glenn that he met you once a while back, but you were involved. I told him that was over and that's when he said he'd be interested in this double-date I'm trying to arrange...if you would just cooperate."

"Kim—"

"Relax. He's fine as hell and just what you need."

"What I need is a job...sans man fan."

"You need both. Look, you told me yourself that you and Luke are never going to happen, and as much as I hoped for that happy ending, I respect your decision to be just friends. But that doesn't mean you get to give up on men altogether. I refuse to let you dry up like you're eighty years old. Not on my watch."

"Kim—"

"And when you finally see Mr. Dunn, you'll thank me," she added. "Trust me...you win twice."

She tried to remember meeting any guys by the name of Jake Dunn, but she had met dozens of fans during the promotional phase of *FleshFX* and never bothered to remember the names of any of them. Stewing quietly, she was more than ready to reject Kim's setup but she reminded herself that the very least she could do was have dinner with the man. "Dinner. That's it. I don't want nor do I need anything else. Got it?"

"Fine." She paused. "One last thing though...you *will* finish packing and ship your shit to my house and live with me until you are able to find a suitable place to stay in Atlanta before starting your job. That is all."

Aris smiled. "You're the bestest, Kim. Really. Thank you."

"Like I said...I always got you."

~ 35 ~

Everything happened just as Kim arranged.

Packed and shipped what little she had to Kim's house...check. Began her search for a suitable and affordable place to rent in Atlanta...check. Dinner with a man she didn't want to meet but was forced to anyway...in progress.

"Well, hello again," Aris said, her eyes wide as Jacob from CMDI approached and leaned in to kiss her cheek in greeting.

"You look incredible," he replied, smiling. "It's great to see you again, Aris."

She wasn't sure how to respond to Jacob formerly known as "Jake" so she redirected her attention to Kim, who was smiling wickedly as she stood next to her boyfriend, Glenn.

"If you'll excuse us?" Aris finally said, pulling Kim out of the living room and down the hall into one of the bedrooms. After closing the door behind them, she turned to face Kim. "I remember him. We met at a party Deena threw for me after I got eliminated from the show. I turned him down cold...this is so awkward."

Kim shook her head. "That was then and this is now. Trust me when I say all that matters to him now is that you're available. Focus on the fun and just relax. First drink is on me...Glen wants to stop by this lounge at some new hotel before we hit the concert, so I'll make sure you're all good and liquored up." She gave Aris a reassuring hug and smiled. "Just enjoy yourself and see where this goes...okay?"

Aris hesitated. Truthfully, she still wasn't over Luke. Maybe she would never be. Who really gets over their first love? Besides, Kim was right. It was time for her to accept reality. Luke was off-limits, and she had to move on. Why not try with Jake? Especially with their paths crossing again in the most bizarre way?

She smiled nervously. "Okay."

"All right," one of the cameramen yelled. "Luke, step a little closer...Jessica, lift your head...yes. Perfect! In three, two, one..."

The flash of the cameras lit up the area as Jessica and Luke posed and smiled. They were celebrating Jessica's crowning achievement in spectacular fashion. Actually, this was just one of several events that were being held in her honor. That's what happened when you became

President of a widely-respected company.

Luke was beyond proud of her. After months of stress and hard work, Jessica's efforts had finally paid off. She'd won the confidence of the Board, and the business community was already abuzz with the news. With Luke's hectic travel schedule, he hadn't been able to attend the other events but he made it a point to join her tonight for this one.

The flashing lights paused for a moment as others moved to stand next to them for another shot. Mrs. Knox approached, giving Luke a sweet smile and a gentle kiss on his cheek, before positioning herself next to Mr. Knox, who shook Luke's hand in greeting.

For so long, Jessica's parents had been parents to him that it felt odd to be standing there as only a friend of the family, instead of a future member of it. He had no regrets, but it was still a bittersweet moment as they all stood and smiled for the camera.

Once the photos were complete, Mrs. Knox walked over to him again and pulled him into a hug.

"It's so good to see you, sweetheart. I'm so glad you could make it." She gave him the type of once-over that only a concerned mother could execute. "You look exhausted...I guess that means things are going very well for you and Devin. Trust me, James wore that same look in the beginning. Just hang in there. It will all pay off."

He nodded, smiling. "We've been up to our necks, but it's much better than the alternative. Things are going exceptionally well. Rest is a luxury these days, but hey...I can sleep when I'm dead."

She laughed. "Well, please know that we are so

proud of you. Don't be a stranger." She kissed him again and glided over to Jessica as Mr. Knox appeared and shook his hand again.

"Luke, I'm hearing great things about you." He patted him on the back and rewarded him with a rare smile. "I spoke to Devin last week. He tells me that you all have landed the Jefferson account."

"Yes, sir. It was iffy for a while, but we got it done."

"Good deal." Looking Luke in the eyes, he nodded. "Keep up the good work. I'm proud of you, son. You know if you ever need anything—"

"Yes, I know, and I appreciate that, sir." He grinned, secretly happy to finally be out from under the man's shadow but forever grateful for the invaluable part he played in his life and career. As easy as it would be to lean on James Knox, Luke was determined to do it all on his own from now on. "But we got this."

Mr. Knox nodded again, a newfound respect and admiration in his eyes. In all the years Luke had worked for the man, he couldn't remember if his former future father-in-law had ever truly regarded him in that way before.

It felt good. Really good.

As they began to chit-chat, Jessica appeared and kissed her father on the cheek. "Now, I know you're not here talking shop, Daddy. Stop drilling Luke, and go grab a drink, dance with Mom, whatever…just do something fun!"

Mr. Knox laughed heartily. "I'm feeling so good tonight, I think I just may twirl your mother around for a bit…she'll probably think I've lost my mind."

"Probably," Jessica and Luke said in unison before

they laughed with him.

Mr. Knox...dancing?

The man really did have a new lease on life.

Luke walked with Jessica over to a group of friends from college who were there to celebrate the occasion. The only one missing was Devin, who was in New York dining with a client, covering for Luke so he could support Jessica tonight. As Jessica launched into an entertaining story from years ago, Luke's phone buzzed.

What were the odds?

Devin.

"Hold on a second, it's loud in here," Luke said, speaking directly into the mouthpiece. He excused himself from the group, leaning in to let Jessica know he was taking a call from Devin. She smiled at him and nodded, turning back to the group and not missing a beat of her story.

When he made it outside the ballroom, Luke brought the phone back up to his ear. "Yeah...what's good?"

"Sounds like it's a real party going on," Devin replied. "How's the turnout?"

"It's packed, dude. Jessica's loving it."

"Good to hear. She deserves it."

"Yeah, she does," Luke replied, bypassing the elevator to take the stairs to the main floor. "But you didn't call for that...I'm guessing this is about the Wilson account. How'd the meeting go?"

As Devin shared the details, Luke strolled through the main lobby of the hotel and listened carefully to his friend's update. He couldn't help the smile that appeared on his face because Devin was basically confirming that they'd just landed their largest account to date. As they excitedly chatted about next steps, Luke ducked into a lounge to avoid having to make small talk with a few of Mr. Knox's associates who were stepping off the elevator and heading in his direction. It was a nice, intimate spot...and a great place to sit for a moment and finish his discussion.

As he walked further inside, his eyes shifted to the small stage where a live band was tuning up for another set. There was a small crowd forming, filling up nearby tables and booths to enjoy the upcoming show. For a moment, he considered going back out into the lobby but decided he'd be done with his conversation before it got loud. Just as he was about to sit in a plush chair in a dark corner, his eyes caught a woman in a backless, black dress. He couldn't see her face, but he didn't need to.

He'd recognize her in that black dress anywhere.

"What the fuck?"

"I said that they want to review the spec next Thursday—"

"Nah," Luke replied, agitated. "Not that. Hey, I need to call you back."

"Everything cool?"

"Aris."

"What?" Devin asked, confused.

"I just spotted her...she's here. I gotta go."

Hanging up the phone, Luke moved quickly across the room determined to get to her. His mind was reeling, wondering how she was even here right now and why she hadn't bothered to call and let him know she was in town.

As he drew closer, Luke finally noticed Kim sitting next to Aris, whispering in her ear before they erupted in laughter. He smiled, glad to see the two friends enjoying themselves...but his smile faded as soon as he saw two men approach and guide both women to a circular booth several feet away, one of the men's hands lingering very low on Aris's bare back.

Luke stopped his pursuit, his jaw clenching.

He was torn. As angry as he was, he had no right to interrupt what was obviously a double date. If Aris had wanted him to know she was in town, she would've told him. So clearly, she had no intention of him knowing at all.

Luke watched as the man leaned in, his hand on Aris's leg as she laughed at whatever bullshit he was spitting in her ear.

"Fuck that," Luke mumbled to himself, seeing red.

He took off in their direction again and didn't slow down until he was standing in front of their booth, his eyes on Aris. Kim noticed him first, gasping before she smiled and shifted her wide eyes to Aris, who was too caught up in New Dude to notice Luke was standing there, watching her.

"Luke," Kim said, a little too loudly. "Hey...it's good to see you."

At the sound of his name, Luke noticed Aris flinch and immediately pull away from her date. When her eyes finally locked with his, he watched several emotions play across her beautiful face before her eyebrows knitted and a frown appeared. The warmth in her eyes turned cold as they shifted to something behind him. Confused, Luke turned to follow her gaze and noticed Jessica approaching him.

Shit.

Kim settled back against the booth, her arms crossed as she shook her head at him. He turned his attention back to Aris, but she was speaking quickly to her date, appearing to be trying to escape the booth.

"Luke, there you are," Jessica said, stopping next to him and placing a hand on his arm. "Mr. and Mrs. Dobson told me they saw you slip in here. I came to get you because there's someone I want you to meet. He's about to leave too, so you must hurry." She turned her head and smiled at everyone. "Hello, I'm so sorry to interrupt." She paused, her eyes finally landing on Aris. "Oh." Moving her hand from Luke's arm, Jessica placed it just below her neck. Recovering quickly, she smiled uneasily at Aris. "Ah...hello, Aris."

No one moved or spoke for several seconds.

"Take your time," Jessica finally said before she walked away. "I'll stall him."

Luke nodded, his eyes never leaving Aris.

"Mood—Aris, can I speak to you for a moment?"

He could feel her date's eyes on him, but he ignored the man's steely gaze. If he knew what was good for him, he'd keep him mouth shut. Aris must have seen something in Luke's eyes because she whispered something to the man and he suddenly shifted out of the booth to help her to her feet.

"Are you sure?" the man asked, the concern in his voice pissing Luke off even more.

"I'm sure. I won't be long."

After saying goodbye to Kim, Luke followed Aris out of the lounge and over to a semi-private area with several plush couches, chairs and coffee tables. Instead of sitting, Aris wrapped her arms around her body, her eyes on everything but him.

She took a deep breath. "Talk."

"What are you doing here?"

She pinned him with a cool gaze, her eyes narrowing. "What are *you* doing here?"

The venom in her voice surprised him, but he continued anyway. "I'm here to support Jessica for her event." His eyes searched her face. "How long have you been in town? Why didn't you call to tell me you were coming?"

She looked away. "I can't do this, Luke."

"What?" he asked confused, reaching out to touch her. When she pulled away from him, he ran a hand over his head in frustration before he looked at her, his eyes pleading. "Will you just talk to me? What's going on? Why didn't you let me know you'd be in town?"

"Jessica has someone for you to meet." She stepped forward, placing a light kiss on his cheek. "You should go do that. Go back to your life, Luke. Goodbye."

"Goodbye?" He watched helplessly as she walked away from him. "Moody, wait...Moody!"

"Just let her go."

He turned and saw Kim standing nearby.

"Let her...what? Hell no." Luke scowled. "No disrespect, Kim...we're cool and all, but this doesn't concern you...so excuse me. I need to go talk to her."

"You will," she replied calmly, forcing him to stop his retreat. "Just not right now. Give her some time."

Cursing, he released a ragged breath and forced himself to relax. Kim was staring at him strangely, a small smile appearing on her face.

"It's not what it looks like, Kim. Jessica and I—"

"I know."

"No, you don't know...and neither does Aris."

"Are you and Jessica still together?"

He held Kim's gaze. "No."

"Good," she replied, her smile broadening. "That's what I thought. Now let me handle the rest."

"Kim—"

"Trust me," she said, patting his arm as walked away. "I want this as much as you do. I'll handle it."

Luke stood quietly for several minutes, internally debating what to do next. He could still go after her. Go back in the lounge and crash their booth again, insist that they talk this out...but what would that do but push Aris further away? He released a colorful string of curses, drawing unwanted attention from people in the vicinity. Ignoring them, Luke nodded to Kim and walked off. Though he wanted to find Aris, he agreed with Kim.

Now was not the time.

When he entered the ballroom, Jessica slipped away from a group of guests she was entertaining and approached him. "I'm sorry about that. How bad is it?"

He laughed without humor. "The worst."

Unable to make sense of it all with an urgent need to vent, Luke confessed everything to Jessica—how he never told Aris that he and Jessica had broken up, how he was trying to give Aris space to focus on her career, how he thought it was best because he needed to get his mind right not to mention that he and Devin were working so much that he barely had time to sleep, never mind trying to start another relationship.

Shaking her head, Jessica grabbed his hand and led him to a roped off area away from the noise and chatter. "Can I be honest?"

He shrugged and looked away, his jaw clenched.

"That is the dumbest thing ever." She shook her head again and sat down on one of the sofas, forcing him to sit with her and relax. "So what are you going to do to fix this?"

That made him grin. Jessica…ever the fixer.

"Look," he began, placing a hand on her knee. "I appreciate you for letting me vent, but we don't have to do this."

"Do what?" She tilted her head, amused. "Be the kind of exes who can talk about their new relationships with each other?"

He glanced at her, skeptically.

"Well, we are." She placed her hand over his and squeezed gently. "Luke, you are my friend and I love you. I'll always love you, but I've had time to accept that we're over and that it really is for the best. It just wasn't meant to be for us, but that doesn't mean that I don't want you to have that life with someone else one day." She laughed as he raised a brow. "Is it really too surprising that I truly want to see you happy?"

He laughed along with her. "You know this shit is awkward as hell, right?"

"Maybe a little…but whatever. I just expect that if I'm ever at a point of fucking up a good thing, you'll be there to talk some sense into me. Promise?"

Smiling, he pulled her into a hug. "Promise."

When he let her go, she searched his eyes, a serious

look on her face. "Stop letting things *just happen* to you, Luke. I can see that you love her but if you want her, you have to go get her. It's time for you to *choose* the life you really want for yourself…don't blow it."

He nodded, the truth of her words sobering him. His entire life had just happened to him at this point all he'd ever done was go along with it, never really knowing who he was and what he really wanted.

Luke rolled his eyes as she grinned at him.

Jessica was *always* right.

Shaking his head, he observed her for several moments before asking, "and what do you really want, Jessica Knox?"

He laughed out loud when she gave him her signature side-eye. He had no doubt of the correct answer to his question, but he still wanted to test his theory anyway. "You want the top spot…Jessica Knox, CEO of Knox Enterprises."

After taking a generous sip of wine, she looked at him and nodded confidently. "You already know…"

~ 36 ~

knock. knock. knock.

Aris ignored Kim's second attempt to make her talk.

They'd gotten home about an hour ago. After making her apologies to Jacob, Aris rushed out of the lounge with the intent to catch a cab. There was no need for her to ruin the rest of the night for Kim, and she refused to ask Jacob to drive her home after she'd all but fallen apart at the sight of her…friend.

Her throat closed up, remembering how quickly she'd gone from joy at seeing Luke to pain when Jessica appeared. She had no right to feel the way she did, no right to harbor anger because she wanted Luke but couldn't have him.

It was that reason that kept her from calling him when she arrived in Dallas. She was only going to be in town for a few weeks, just long enough to get her ducks in a row and plan her move to Atlanta. But she knew that a few weeks was all it would take for her to slip back into a place she didn't want to be. It had taken her three times as long to scale back her calls and texts to Luke after Comic-Con, to stop needing him and wanting him so badly. If she had called him, they would have spent her few weeks in Dallas the way they always had when she lived there…together.

How was either of them supposed to move on when neither refused to let go?

Sitting up, she wiped her face. Her mistake had always been in her belief that they could be the friends they were before love got in the way. Her throat closed up again just as Kim resumed her knocking in an attempt to get her to open the door and talk.

She and Luke could never be friends. They could never be anything other than what they were supposed to be…which was what they *couldn't* be. Pretending otherwise was futile. It wouldn't work, and it hurt too much to try.

So there was only one thing left for her to do.

She had to—completely—let him go.

After taking a few deep breaths, Aris walked over to unlock and open the door. Noticing the worried look on Kim's face, she tried to fake a smile. It didn't work.

Turning on her heel, Aris returned to her bed and pulled the covers up to her neck. "I don't want to talk about it."

"You don't have to, honey," Kim said as she pulled back the covers on the other side of the bed and climbed in beside her. "But I'm here anyway."

~ 37 ~

HALLOWEEN

Aris hadn't paid a single minute of attention to the movie on her television screen. From the moment she'd turned it on and camped out on her sofa, she had been distracted--replaying her first week of work over and over in her mind, worrying about the impression she made and whether or not moving to Atlanta had been the right decision. Despite having returned to Georgia, which was the last thing she'd ever imagined she'd do, so far it felt like Atlanta was her best move, but something still felt off and she'd been consumed with anxiety since the day she left Dallas a few weeks ago.

"Always forward," she mumbled to herself.

Just as she was finally getting into the movie, she heard a few hard knocks at her front door. It was easy to ignore whomever it was the first time, but when the idiot began another series of knocks, she rolled her eyes, paused the movie and counted to five. The person was still knocking when she finally snatched the door open with her face twisted into an angry scowl that quickly give way to a look of complete surprise.

"Luke?"

He stared at her silently.

She slammed the door in his face.

"Moody...Moody, open the door...Moody!"

Racing back to the sofa to grab the phone, she heard more knocking as she dialed. Kim answered on the first ring, of course.

"Yeeesss?" Kim answered sarcastically.

"What did you do?!"

"I'm helping you."

She wanted to throw something. "How many times do I have to tell you that I don't need your help!"

"Yes, Aris...you really do."

"I don't have time for this shit, Kim...how the hell could you tell him where I lived? Did you tell him to come over here too?"

"He's there now?" Kim asked, sounding as surprised as she was. "I was hoping he would avoid the phone and go the in-person route. Smart man."

"Next time I see you," she said, venom lacing her voice. She'd had about enough of Kim's meddling ass, of Luke's games...of everything. "Ass. Kicked."

"Yeah, whatever. Now go answer the damn door." Kim laughed. "You know you want to."

"No, I do not! What about me trying to move on did you not understand? Why would you do this to me?"

"Because you need to finish this. Just hear him out,

Aris. If after what he says you decide to stick with your I'm-single-and-loving-it-plan then fine. But it's time you two stop running from each other and *talk*."

She cursed. "I hate you."

Kim chuckled. "You'll love me later."

Aris hung up without saying goodbye, Kim's amusement at her situation pissing her off more than Luke's incessant knocking on her front door.

Marching back into the foyer, she snatched the door open for the second time and glared at him before turning around and walking away. She hadn't made it to the sofa before he was standing in her path, his eyes serious but pleading.

Crossing her arms, she tilted her head and raised an eyebrow. "Why are you here?"

"I love you."

Her eyes narrowed and her nostrils flared as she stepped forward to get in his face. "Don't you dare—"

"Stop," he said, placing a finger against her lips. "Just listen to me. Can you do that? Please?"

She pushed his finger away and twisted her mouth, careful to give him another dose of serious attitude before conceding.

"I broke up with Jessica—"

"You what?" she asked, her eyes growing wide again. "When did—"

He sighed. "Are you going to let me talk or not?"

Not. Inhaling deeply, she flared her nostrils again before forcing a tight smile. "Fine. I'm *listening*."

He watched her for a while, a slight smile on his lips. "Damn, I've missed you so much, it's *crazy*…"

"Not now," she snapped though his admission made

her soul dance. "Talk."

"Jessica and I broke up months ago," he continued. "I quit my job at Knox Corp shortly after. I didn't have to, but I realized that I needed to know who I really was without her and her family's name behind me. I decided to go into business with Devin and, after much debate, we finally decided the best place to start up was in Atlanta." He held up both hands to ward off her expected response as soon as she twisted her lips at his way-too-convenient news. "Devin's last business was in Midtown before he sold it, and he's still very well connected in the city's tech scene. Plus, I got family on the east side so it made sense to be here. Permanently."

She stepped back, her brows knitting together as she processed everything he'd told her. "You *live* here?"

"For the record," he replied, his eyes dancing. "I was living here before you showed up." When her mouth fell open, he laughed. "Not in this neighborhood, but I do live here now. Across town in Dunwoody."

"But when she showed up in the hotel lounge looking for you, like you two were still together, I thought—"

"I know what you thought. That night, Jessica was being honored at an event celebrating her recent promotion. I was there to support her...as a *friend*. That's it."

"Then why didn't you say anything?" When he raised an eyebrow, she shook her head. "Not that night. Why didn't you tell me what's been going on with you when we were in San Diego?"

"It wasn't the right time. My relationship with Jessica was over, yes...but things were still so complicated. I really needed to get my shit together first. Emotionally and professionally. That way, when I finally told you everything, you would see and know that the past is behind me, where it belongs, and that I am my own man. You deserved that. *We* deserved that."

"Deserved what?"

He grinned at her and reached up to gently press a finger against the wrinkle between her eyebrows until the skin smoothed. "A fresh start."

Backing away, he turned and walked out of her apartment. A few minutes later, he strolled in with two big brown paper bags.

"I already ate," she lied as he passed her.

He gave her the side-eye. "You're always hungry."

Crossing her arms and twisting her mouth again, she watched him pulled out pancakes, smoked sausage, country ham, fried apples, grits, bacon, eggs and hash browns. After a few trips to carry everything and arrange it on the coffee table in her living room, he settled onto the sofa and waved her over to join him. When she finally sat next to him, he reached for her hand and she placed it in his, closing her eyes as he prayed over the food.

When she opened her eyes, she turned to face him. "I am, you know."

He raised an eyebrow as began to scoop strawberry jelly into his grits. "You're what?"

"Proud of you."

Glancing at her, he smiled. "That means a lot coming from you, Moody."

"And I mean every word," she said, smiling. "I know it couldn't have been easy to strike out on your own, but you did it. You're *doing* it...and it looks good on you. Despite the bags under your eyes."

"Always with the jokes," he replied, laughing with her. "But yeah. Your man's been pretty busy...making moves, losing sleep, working hard. It's necessary, but I've also lost a lot of precious time. Which is why I'm here now, trying to make everything up to you with a delicious, deep-fried, artery-clogging breakfast."

She stopped chewing her pancakes when she heard his casual reference to him being her man. When she turned to look at him, he was watching her intently.

"If you'll let me," he added, reading her mind.

"Let you do what exactly?" she mumbled, trying hard to swallow.

"Be your man. Make it up to you. Make love to you. *Love you*...for as long as you'll have me."

"You and me?"

"All of me and all of you. All of the time."

She observed him for a long while before leaning over and giving him a sweet, syrupy kiss. "I'm all in."

For the next hour, a series of questions and answers bounced between them as they ate and caught up on their work lives and family lives and everything in between. After finishing their food and placing their empty plates on the coffee table, Luke spread his arms wide. Grabbing the remote, Aris curled up against him and placed her head against his chest.

When she pressed PLAY to continue the movie, the dark screen came to life and Luke laughed, pulling her closer and kissing the top of her head.

"*Hope Floats*?" Luke asked.

Aris looked up at him and smiled. "Hope floats."

ACKNOWLEDGMENTS

I have so many feelings right now as I am writing this. I am so grateful to complete this journey and share my fifth novel with you. Wow, number 5. The significance of that is not lost on me. I am humbled to have done this one more time...praise be to God.

Special thanks to the first readers of this story— Sharon, Shakir, Diego, Coty, Linda, Steve, Gloria, Tiffani, Denise, Rod, Shonda and T'wana—I appreciate all of you more than you could ever know. From my heart, thank you for your time, interest, feedback, encouragement and enthusiasm. You are the BEST! ❤

And to YOU, the reader—thank you so much for giving me a chance and supporting my dream. I am truly grateful.

Peace and Blessings,

RL

About the Author

Rae Lamar is a mild-mannered consultant by day and fiction writer by night who calls Atlanta home. She is also author of *22, UNLIKE ME, SOMEWHERE IN BETWEEN* and *OPEN*. To learn more about Rae, visit raelamar.com.